BOOK THREE IN THE IDEA MAN TRILOGY

I0633245

THE
TRUE
MAN

a novel

KRISTIN HELLING

THE TRUE MAN
by Kristin Helling

Printed in the United States of America
First Printing, 2020

ISBN-13: 978-1-946921-16-1

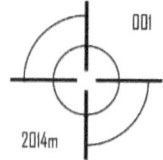

ADRENALINE

Adrenaline
An imprint of Wordwraith Books, LLC
705-B SE Melody Lane #149
Lee's Summit, MO 64063
e-mail *wordwraiths@gmail.com*
website *www.wordwraiths.com*

Edited by J. R. Frontera
Cover Design by Deranged Doctored Designs
Format Design by Rod Galindo
Proofread by Wayne Burnop

Kristin's email *author@kristinhelling.com*
Kristin's website *kristinhelling.com*

The Library of Congress Cataloging-in-Publication Data is
available upon request.

BOOKS BY
KRISTIN HELLING

All books available on Amazon.com

THE IDEA MAN TRILOGY
(comedic, suspense thriller)
The Idea Man
The Marked Man
The True Man

THE MASTERMIND MURDERERS SERIES
(psychological, crime thriller)
The Altruism Effect
The Bystander Effect
The Carbon Effect
The Domino Effect

STANDALONE SERIES
(soft sci fi Thriller)
Capsule

For Austin & Remington,
Mom & Dad,
The Wordwraiths,
and Indiepub.

TABLE OF CONTENTS

ONE

GREYSEN

The drowsy sensation that coursed through his veins hadn't even worn off yet before he went back for more. Greysen paced to the door and tugged the knob. *Still locked.* He returned to the slightly reclined bed, with a tray next to it containing needles, sticky dot electrodes, and the memory machine's spider-looking head contraption. A computer was set up next to the bed, too, with a blank vitals tracking graph on its screen.

He needed to hurry if he was to do this off the books.

Why do I have to ask permission? I'm the boss now, right? His hands gravitated towards his hair and he laced his fingers through it. Then pulled. He winced. A sharp headache followed. He let go of his hair and patted his cheeks with his hands.

His inner monologue wouldn't shut up. *Conflicting motives. Arguable sense of guilt. Why do I feel like I still have to answer to someone? I finally worked my way to the head of this company and I still don't feel like it's mine. If I say I can do this process for however long I want and by myself if I want to, then I can! But then there's protocol...*

There was a specific protocol for a reason, after all: Nobody was to use the memory machine alone. Vitals must be monitored by a second person.

When Greysen had drawn up plans for this device years back, he'd always put each invention through what he'd liked to call, "NASA-ing the project". Whenever NASA launched a rocket, they went through tests. Their goal was to specifically find a reason, any reason at all, why they *couldn't* launch. If they couldn't find a single reason, then the mission would be a go.

Greysen had decided to adopt this method when creating his inventions. And the memory machine had not passed that test. Not even by a long shot. Yet here he was, in this lab at Humavision headquarters, confronted with the endless possibilities of the technology. He was still so conflicted as to whether or not it was a good idea to engage. One of the number of reasons he hadn't wanted to bring it to fruition was the simple fact that a man could lose himself in it. It was easy to become wrapped up in the memories, wallowing in the past, and Greysen was aware of the ability to waste time when hooked up to the memory machine.

And in this case, he could also lose the former love of his life, Molly… again. She'd made him promise he wouldn't even *begin* to dive into Edrick's memory data.

Edrick. The man who'd killed himself and left his company to Greysen in his will. Greysen's ex-boss; whom he'd wanted nothing more than to see dead, was now dead.

And if Greysen was ever going to prove to the people who now worked for him that he was a worthy boss, he needed to see first-hand what he was up against, right? Through the eyes of the person who'd owned this business before him.

Not to mention the fact that Edrick hadn't actually been the boss at all, it appeared. Edrick had answered to someone else. Only this "higher up" wasn't an owner or shareholder of the company at all. At least not legally. Greysen had seen the paperwork when it was handed over to him. There'd been lawyers present and everything. He needed to get to the bottom of that, as well. His company... his *life* depended on it.

Greysen continued to pace. He hadn't showered for days, had been functioning on very little sleep, had been obsessed over every single detail he'd experienced in Edrick's memories. He was headed right toward that destiny of losing himself, just like he'd initially feared all those years ago.

But... he *had* to know.

It wasn't a matter of discussion anymore. He was thinking too much, and that was never a good thing. No, he'd done quite enough thinking. So he shut off his mind. Shut off the thoughts. Shut off the worry. He was just going to do it.

Greysen rushed over to the cabinet and pulled out the kit he needed to do the job. He ripped it open and quickly assembled the bag of liquid onto the IV stand. After situating it, he placed the cap on his head that had all the wires coming out of it. He turned to the computer and logged in.

His gaze shot to the door. Paranoia crept into him. It was dangerous for him to go under, alone. Last time he'd tried this, Carrie was there to monitor his vitals, and even though he'd told her not to take him back out of the memories until he'd wanted to, she had, anyway. She'd told him it was because his vitals had shot to extreme and dangerous levels. But what would have happened if she hadn't taken him out of it early? He'd known what he'd experienced was intense, but he needed to get through those memories. He was motivated to get through them.

Carrie had expressed concern for his health shortly after that and she'd made him promise he would take a break.

So, naturally, his only response was to say yes to her, so she'd leave him alone. Then, he'd snuck behind her back into this very lab.

The computer unlocked obediently with his passcode, and he inserted the chip he'd kept in a carrying case in his pocket. Once the interface was ready to go, vital charts up and all, he took his place on the bed. He laid back and connected the wires from the headset to the computer. Then, he took the IV needle attached to the clear bag of serum that hung from a metal stand.

As he hovered the needle over his forearm, the thought haunted him again. *Should I really be doing this alone?* Carrie had already told him it wasn't a smart idea. But perhaps she wasn't talking about the mental side of it. She was a very scientific and logical person. Perhaps she was saying it wasn't biologically safe to do it alone.

But he was here. He was all set up and ready to go. There was no turning back now.

TWO

GREYSEN

It was that sickly feeling again. The one where his muscles seized up as though he were paralyzed. Limbs heavy, and all the unused energy coursed through his veins at an exponential rate. But his focus wasn't on how he felt, it was now on the scene in which Greysen stood.

In an office in front of a computer, Greysen looked down at his arms and hands. Though they weren't his own. His perspective was through the eyes of his ex-boss. The only thing that remained of him, now.

"No, no, no don't hang up!" Edrick pleaded with someone on his computer screen.

Greysen perked up. Perhaps this was the 'higher up' again. Perhaps this time in the memory, the person Edrick answered to wouldn't be cast in shadow. Greysen might be able to catch a glimpse of him this time, which was really one of the goals he'd intended from the beginning when immersing himself in these memories, after all. *Immersing... or losing myself?*

"I finally got through to you. It's been very difficult thus far. Please, I just have a few questions for you," Edrick urged on.

Questions about what? Why does he have to answer to this other person? What's he going to have Edrick do? What happens if the black and white instructions present a gray area?

"Okay..." The person who responded was female. She was reluctant.

Greysen was taken aback. *Wait... now there's a woman involved, too? What is the meaning of all this?*

"I need to know what your connection to Greysen Price is? You recognize that name, don't you? I can tell by the expression on your face that you recognize it very well."

Greysen's attention focused even more at the mention of his name. He felt a sleazy, slimy film crawl over his own emotions. *Edrick's feelings in the memory.*

"Why do you need that information? Is Greysen in trouble?"

At that moment, it clicked. The female. Her voice was more familiar than he'd ever imagined. But how could it be her? And why? It'd been years and years since he'd heard her voice. He squinted at the computer screen in front of Edrick, focusing in on it again for the first time since arriving in this particular memory.

Sure enough, Greysen's guess was confirmed. His heart leapt for joy and sunk with sadness all at the same time. It wasn't the 'higher up' he had been hoping for. But this memory was important for other reasons: it was Dottie Herring.

Of course her name was different now, being married and all. But when he'd known her, it had been Herring. She was much, much older here in this memory, but more beautiful than ever. He reached out as though he could touch her, though inside he knew that was stupid. Not only was this a memory, but it was also the virtual version of Dottie inside a memory that was not even his own.

They'd lost touch, right around the time they'd graduated high school. She was his first love, or so he'd thought. He'd been over-the-moon smitten by her. But all of that had come crashing down that early summer. And after that, she'd taken off. She'd never contacted him again. She'd never even said goodbye. Yet here she was, talking to Edrick, and the tone of her voice was worried. Worried for *him*. And she seemed to be protecting him.

But they'd lost touch until recently...

Greysen's heart pattered in his chest, strong enough to be apparent over the fog of emotions he'd taken on from inside the memory.

How could Edrick know to try and get a hold of Dottie? Why was he investigating Greysen's life in the first place?

Greysen looked around Edrick's office as best he could. A calendar, a clock. There had to be *something* that could indicate to him what year this memory took place.

"Yes. He's in a lot of... danger," Edrick responded.

"Danger?" her voice shot back.

Greysen's gaze shot up and saw her looking back and forth over her shoulder.

She appeared paranoid. Probably watching out for her family or others to make sure nobody saw her on the webcam. "Well, I can assure you that I have no clue where he is."

She was telling the truth. Greysen hadn't told her where he was located.

He thought about the recent contact they'd had. Before he'd gone back to Chicago when Parker was taken from the cabin, he'd sent a

12

package to Dottie. A heart locket necklace. On the anniversary of their first date.

Was it inappropriate because she'd been married and it'd been years since their last contact? Probably. But it was important to him. He thought he was in imminent danger at the time. It could have been his only chance. And now, *she* was in danger. *Because of me.*

"I think you're lying." Edrick purred. He leaned forward, closer to the camera lens. "I think me and my men need to pay you a little visit."

Greysen tensed. *What the hell, Asshole?* He had to keep reminding himself that Edrick had gotten what he deserved in the end. And that if something terrible had happened to Dottie because of him, he most definitely would have heard about it by now. He never would've sent the package to her if he'd known she'd become a target.

But even if the worst fate didn't happen to Dottie, Edrick was still poking around, and still threatening her. And the principle of that matter was the fact that when Greysen had disappeared, these Humavision criminals had done any and everything to try to track him down. They'd torn apart and intruded on the privacy of his entire life.

Greysen had always prided himself on his private life. It appeared that once he went undercover and escaped the country, he'd forfeited that privacy. Not just his everyday life, his home, Molly, his job, but also his past. And very, very sensitive parts of his past.

He observed the pain in Dottie's eyes. A pain that came from the depths inside her, and he couldn't tell if it was regret for having ever known him, or regret for letting him slip away.

He'd had enough of this shit. Every time he dived into Edrick's memories, he learned more about the situation, but less about what he was actually surfing the memories to find. He was exhausted. Exhausted from the physical and mental toll it was taking on his body, exhausted from not getting anywhere quick enough. He wasn't any closer to finding who Edrick had answered to. To finding the true heart of this company, the one he hated so much, but still yearned to discover so much about it. Surely, if there was someone out there who Edrick had to answer to, they would reach out to Greysen eventually. He could just sit around and wait for that, couldn't he?

No, he wanted to be proactive. The sooner he found out about who was in charge, the sooner he could stop being haunted by it.

As Greysen closed his eyes in the memory, ready to come back out of it, he felt like he was falling. It was as if he'd taken a step in the dark, thinking there was one more step to take, only the step wasn't there. His stomach sank. He jolted awake.

He was still in the office. Still inside Edrick's perspective.

And then the thought occurred to him. *There's nobody on the other side to unhook the serum. I'm on my own. I'm... trapped. Inside these memories.* The panic stirred. His heart ached as it pounded out of his chest. Then the sweat. The shaking. "Calm... down..."

The fragmented memories shifted.

He could only imagine what his vitals looked like on the screen outside in the real world. *What was I thinking? Why did I never think of this side effect happening before I went under?*

Because there had always been at least two people manning the machine. Nobody had ever had a reason to take the risk alone.

He'd been stupid.

He regretted it.

And the overall general fear arose that perhaps he wouldn't make it out of this thing alive. Of all the situations he'd been in in his life, this would be the thing that was going to end him. Wouldn't it?

Before he could spend another moment thinking about the worst, the memory shift completed. Edrick was in his mansion now.

Greysen seemed to be spiraling through random memories, uncontrolled, with no way to read it from left to right, or in chronological order. He'd designed the machine to cross-reference what was in the viewer's head with what was in the memories. That way he could sort of direct the viewing… but he'd panicked.

So now the memories were spinning out of control… And apparently there was no way to influence what direction they traveled if he panicked.

The scene presented now was Edrick, in a bedroom, with a naked woman tied to his bed frame.

Greysen closed his eyes to the memory. *My god, Edrick, really?*

Was this consensual? He didn't recognize the woman from the split second he'd seen her face. Relief washed over him that it wasn't Molly. Or Dottie, for that matter. He didn't know what Edrick had done with her and he knew he ran the risk of having to watch those memories too.

But right now, Greysen wanted to be anywhere other than here. This place... the memories that surrounded it... Greysen had never been in this room before, but it was the feeling of the whole house. He'd recognized it right away because of the structure and the style.

Greysen heard the sounds of Edrick and the woman beneath him. She didn't sound like she was particularly enjoying it, but then another sound would arise that challenged that notion. Maybe she'd *had* to do this? Maybe she'd had no other way out but to pretend. Who would ever want to be with Edrick on an intimate level by choice?

Perhaps there was that higher-up who was motivating him to do horrible things to the people around him, but then there were also situations like this particular memory. Nobody was instructing Edrick to act on his impulses here. He did these little side projects all the time on his own.

Greysen became increasingly uncomfortable. Wishing he could change the memory, wishing he could be anywhere other than here. Nausea crept up his throat as he felt trapped. He tried to direct his thoughts somewhere else. What time frame was it right now? Could it be possible that he was brought to this memory because he'd somehow directly influenced it?

And just like that, the noises subsided. He couldn't tell if they were done, or something had happened to stop it.

"I said not to answer the door for anyone," Edrick sneered.

Greysen cautiously opened his eyes to see what was happening. Edrick got up out of the bed and started to pull his briefs and pants back on.

Who was he talking about? Who had answered the door? Other people were in the mansion with him?

Corin. Could he be talking about Corin? Was this memory before Greysen had met her?

Edrick went to the door, then turned back toward the woman. "You stay put. Oh, right..." Greysen could feel the smile on Edrick's lips, knew it had to be that terrible, awful toothy grin he hated so much. "... you aren't going anywhere."

The woman yanked at the restraints. "Hey, you... wait... don't leave me—at least give me something to cover up with," she pleaded. Her voice was not sexy and seductive like Edrick's body language suggested.

18

Greysen felt bad for her. Edrick was just going to leave this butt-naked, vulnerable woman tied to his bed? It wasn't below him. But Greysen was just happy he could get out of that bedroom for a moment. Edrick went out the door and down the hall.

The woman yelled behind them, but as soon as the door slammed, it was as though the room itself was sound proof. They couldn't hear a thing.

This was a part of the mansion that Greysen didn't remember. He went with the memory of Edrick, embodied within that horrible man, down a set of stairs into what soon became familiar. A front foyer. Multiple rooms. No sign of Corin. Edrick slowed, listening stealthily. He rounded the corner onto this door and pushed it open, standing in the door frame.

There was a man in the next room. Greysen narrowed his eyes, trying to identify the person. Then the man turned around and Greysen's heart sank.

It was *himself*. Standing in the library in Edrick's mansion, looking in their direction.

It was surreal to see himself standing there, a shell of a man. It didn't take even a moment for him to realize at what part of his life this scene took place. It was in the beginning... before

19

everything happened. If he could have known then what he knew now... everything would have been different. And though the person standing on the other side of the room was him, he was so far away now from who he'd used to be, emotionally. This guy was much younger, with yes, a lot of experience, but still far less than he had now.

Aside from these thoughts, he immediately jerked into a different emotion, and not one of his own. He felt frustrated as he looked at this little punk in front of him. *Himself*. What was going on? Ah... yes. He was not inside his own mind. He was inside Edrick's. Boy, he was sick of being inside this head.

Another feeling approached. This one was more complicated. One that Greysen hadn't expected to feel. It wasn't hatred... it was... fear? *It was fear.* Edrick was afraid of him. He was damn good at hiding it. It had never occurred to Greysen that Edrick could ever fear him at any given moment. Perhaps this vulnerability was why Edrick hadn't wanted anyone looking through his memories? Was ego enough of a reason, besides the obvious breech of privacy? Greysen had always thought it had to run deeper than that. Right? It had to be some kind of secret within the company. Or perhaps something to do with the fact that he answered to some secret boss, which Greysen had discovered through these memories very quickly.

"You ready to talk business?" Edrick asked, and the memory Greysen wheeled around. It appeared like he was staring right into him.

"That's why I'm here," memory Greysen answered.

That feeling of fear was still there, but it was masked with arrogance. "Very well. That's a nasty wound on your back, I can see it through your shirt."

Edrick referred to the wound left by the hooks from the taser Greysen had endured not more than a few hours before in this memory.

Greysen watched the scene unfold, the scene he knew all too well, because, well, he'd experienced it. And he wasn't too keen on experiencing it another time. He loathed being in that house again. And as Edrick spoke that sentence, it felt as though the scars on his back were re-ripped open, despite the years and years that had passed since this day in the mansion.

Greysen, though bogged down by Edrick's feelings, which were beginning to bore him and overwhelm him just the same, spaced out of the conversation. Though when he heard the name *Molly*, it all flooded back. *Molly*. He'd forgotten that he'd learned much later that Molly was also in that mansion at that same time. If only he could wander around a memory, instead of being restricted to the scenes Edrick belonged in. Perhaps this was where he'd learn more about why she didn't want him watching the memories.

The details of all that happened next were as clear as the day they had actually happened. He didn't need a memory to relive that. But to be able to snap in the missing pieces was enlightening. The parts where Edrick was knocked out, by Greysen, were fuzzy. As though the memory had lines through it. White noise. Interference. But Greysen didn't need to see those parts anyway. He'd lived it.

It was when Edrick woke up again that Greysen was most interested in. As Edrick discovered the mess that was now the back-up control room, panic set in. Hyperventilation. Difficulty to think, and breath, and feel. It was torturous. And Greysen wanted out, mostly because he was influenced by how Edrick felt.

He could feel the man's panicked thoughts: Should he run away? Should he face the truth? Should he find Greysen first? Yes. That one.

Edrick ran through the hall, banging into walls. He stopped at a room with a wooden home décor sign above the door that read, *The Armory*.

Greysen had a brief thought about what might possibly be in there. Perhaps he labeled his mancave that? Just as quickly as he wondered about it, Edrick burst through the door.

It was not a mancave. What control Greysen had of his own thoughts went wild. *It's literally an armory. Because who* doesn't *have an armory in their house?*

Edrick ran his hand along a row of rifles, ending on the last one. But instead of picking it up, he turned to a black-draped box and pulled off the cloth. Three hounds stood inside the large kennels he had exposed, the whites of their eyes piercing in the dim room.

The dogs in the woods. Greysen tried to keep the timeline of this memory conscious in his mind.

The poor canines had probably been trained to hunt and kill. Greysen only hoped their usual sport didn't involve humans. But one could not be so certain when it came to Edrick.

Edrick opened the cages, guiding each of the three dogs out on a chain attached to their collars.

Greysen's vision and mind became a blur as the memory guided him through the mansion to glass double-doors that exited off the kitchen.

Edrick hissed words in Spanish to the dogs, then released them. He brushed his palms on his pants and lifted his hand to his head.

Greysen felt the grogginess. The dull, aching headache. Was it his physical body on the outside coming through, or was this how Edrick felt—effects of his head injury inflicted by Greysen?

Edrick didn't stall. He bolted out of the kitchen, back up the stairs. He tore for the master bedroom, pulling open the doors.

The woman he'd left in his bed was gone. Edrick didn't love her. She was a toy. That much was evident in the greasy, gross feelings Greysen currently squirmed in.

"Shit!" Edrick yelled, looking around as if she might be hiding like a child. "Oh... no no no." He ran for it. Faster than he had to find Greysen.

He turned around, back down the hall. It seemed like there were so many doors. When Edrick got to the one door that was already cracked open, he swung it back. The cage... that sat there in the bare room was empty. Halfway out of the cage lay a blanket that had been dragged out. A little farther from that were

24

broken handcuffs. This cage was not for another animal. It was for a human.

Panic struck even more so than when he was in the control room. Greysen felt as though he'd burst with this new-found emotion. He couldn't handle it. It was just unbearable. Exhausting.

And the thought came into his mind, clearly from the thoughts of Edrick within that memory: The girl in his master bedroom was gone, yes. But she could have only been let go by one person. The one person that was supposed to be locked up in this cage for later.

The only other person Greysen knew of who was in that mansion during this same timeline... was Molly.

Greysen blacked out. Then, searing pain.

It took several moments for him to realize where he was, as the room around him came back into view. He was in the small surgical room within the Humavision building. In the present. Back to himself and out of Edrick's head.

Memories. Edrick's memories.

The searing pain came from his wrist, which he'd clearly landed on wrong when he'd fallen from the bed. His experience must have been so intense that it made him physically lurch off the bed, ripping the serum IV out of his arm as he fell, then landing on his wrist.

He couldn't see protruding bone. That was the good thing. But it was most likely sprained, based on the amount of throbbing pain that came from it. He looked up at the serum bag and realized it still had half the amount of liquid in it. He would have continued to be trapped in those memories for far longer if it hadn't been for his physiological response.

That had saved him. He didn't know what would have happened otherwise. He tried to stand, but his legs were like Jell-O. Floppy and weak, a symptom of going under. He was able to reach up and pull the sheets of recorded paper off the machine. He studied them, as he had with others before. He found the part where he had experienced the most trauma. It was apparent, right there on the page. He'd had a seizure. That was what had made him fall out of the seat. Why his body was so clenched and sore. He dropped the papers.

I shouldn't be alive right now! He was exhausted. If only he'd just allow himself to doze off for just a small minute and regain some energy, so he could continue his quest.

He regretted watching those memories without supervision.

But he'd seen two things that were so important to pursue. One was Dottie. Was she in danger? That memory of them was when Edrick and Dottie were older. It wasn't when Greysen had first fled the country. It was more recent. He hadn't seen or spoken to Dottie in years, though he did have one small little secret about Dottie that he'd never thought he'd have to reveal.

The second thing was that Molly had escaped the mansion that night herself, and she'd taken the woman who'd been chained to Edrick's bed with her. Either that or it was the other way around. Regardless, her journey had started that day as well. Just like it had for Greysen. He wondered what else she'd been through while he was away, and he wasn't entirely sure he wanted to know.

THREE

PARKER

Parker rolled over on the bed to find it empty. Blurry-eyed and groggy, he reached for his phone and checked the time. 10am. Noriana was already at work. She'd gotten up early every day of the week for her job at the museum. Parker didn't need to work. He'd been living off the book advance for quite some time now, and even though he was still writing, at least he didn't have to feel the pressure of wasting his time at a "day job", taking more time away from writing. Even if he wasn't currently selling his work, he was still always working on *something*.

But the days were beginning to mesh together. And it was getting harder and harder to wake up before 9am. Sometimes he'd get a text from Noriana to meet him for lunch, and he'd still be in his boxers with unwashed hair.

He got up and moved to the window. Pulling the curtains back, he peered out onto the road below. A fresh blanket of white had covered the walks overnight. As he looked at the new-fallen snow, he couldn't help but think of his own new beginning. It was a new opportunity. A fresh start. A blank slate. He could move on. Start anew. Make whatever kind of life he wanted to make.

He had a beautiful girlfriend. He was in the most beautiful and romantic city in the world. Creativity, inspiration, and history surrounded him at every turn. It was as though every time his life became quiet, uneventful, and just plain normal, he craved adventure again.

Parker got dressed and left their apartment. He followed the sidewalk, on the hunt for breakfast. He only had a few euros in his pocket, so he decided to stop by an ATM on the way. He always preferred to pay via notes, or cash, instead of a card so that he could visually see the money he spent. He looked back and forth over his shoulder, an action of habit, and then slipped his card into the ATM's card slot. He typed in his numbers.

Denied.

"What?" Maybe he'd punched in the wrong number. He tried again.

Denied.

The only reason why it could be denied was if he didn't have the funds available to withdraw them. *How can this be? There should be a balance in there!* He'd received more than half a million dollars in advance money for his last book. Sure, he had been living off it for quite some time, and sure, the exchange rate from dollars to euro would have brought the overall value down, but not by a drastic amount.

Was I robbed? He racked his mind for any situation that may have put him in such a position. *Did I leave my card out at a bar or restaurant somewhere? Digital fraud?* He pulled out his phone and opened up his online banking app. When he brought up the account, his heart sank.

"I'm... broke?" he whispered. It took all he had not to drop his phone on the street. The feeling was nauseating. He had no money. He was broke. A deadbeat. *As always.*

Noriana was out there making a living doing her dream job, and here he was. Broke AF. No job. Could he call writing a job when he wasn't making any money doing it, and he'd spent more time procrastinating than writing the next book? And now that the advance was gone, he had nothing left.

31

He thought about Greysen back in the States, also living his dream job running the company he'd once left all those years ago. After Greysen assumed ownership of the company and before Parker moved to Paris, Greysen had offered him a job copywriting for Humavision. At the time, Parker had turned it down.

Of course. Right? Why would he ever work for Greysen's company? He didn't belong there. His life when Greysen was involved was chaos. And anyway, he couldn't justify leaving Noriana. She'd put up with all the danger lately... put up with *him*, too, and his lack of productivity. His lack of inspiration.

But, and he'd gone through this over and over in his head, if it weren't for Greysen and that first note he'd left on his rental car all that time ago, he never would have gone to the museum, and he never would have met Nori. Greysen was responsible for some of the worst things that had ever happened to him, but he was also responsible for one of the best things.

Perhaps he should reconsider that offer for the copywriting job, if it was still on the table. It was worth a shot asking, at least.

Parker put his head down and shoved his bank card back in his wallet. After that news, he couldn't fathom spending anything on

32

breakfast. He headed back to the apartment. Toast would be fine. He liked toast.

Though there was something else back in their apartment that he was drawn to first.

When he got back, he knelt down under the bed and pulled out a wooden box. It was the place where he'd put his memories and keepsakes. It was also special because of the fact that this was the only thing that was his, alone. Something that Nori didn't share ownership in. And he'd put it for safekeeping under the bed, as though it were some hidden-away secret. She know about the box, of course, but it didn't really concern her. It was his. And she respected that.

He opened the box and reached in for a small bag. It was velvet, with woven silk drawstrings. He pulled the puckered seal apart and poured the contents of the bag out in his hand.

It was a ring. An engagement ring. A small yellowish diamond center, with smaller diamonds surrounding it in a halo. The band was gold, but tarnished in the most beautiful way. It was his mother's. She'd given it to him when he'd told her he was moving to Paris to be with Noriana.

33

When they'd had that conversation, his mom had told him she'd never seen such happiness painted on his face as she'd seen right then.

He stared down at the glint of shimmer from the big diamond.

I could pawn it... He laughed in spite of himself at the fact that had never, and would never, be an option with the heirloom he held in his hand.

Was it too soon to propose to Nori? Would she say yes?

He had no doubt in his mind that he wanted to be with her. Perhaps proposing to her right before he broke the news that he was going to Chicago to work for Greysen might lessen the blow. It seemed like a good plan. Of course every time he thought he had a good plan, it always backfired.

Perhaps this time would be different. Perhaps...

FOUR

PARKER

P arker swiped sweaty palms against his pants and sucked in a deep breath, trying to calm the wild racing of his heart. He walked into the museum like he had the last few nights he'd come to prepare, only this time it was different. This time, he could be leaving with a fiancé. And that was the question: *Why was he so nervous?* Quite possibly because he was going to be asking the love of his life to marry him... or was it the possibility that she could potentially say no? Judging by the way things had been going for their relationship, he couldn't imagine her saying no. He was probably overthinking everything, just like he always did. This was something serious, something that would change the course of their entire lives.

The ring was heavy in his pocket, but not as heavy as the way his heart felt inside his chest.

He would follow up this proposal with the news that Greysen had confirmed he still had a job available for Parker. And that Parker had accepted it. That whole idea put a damper on things, sure. Regardless, it would be better to look at it as today was one day, and the job matter was going to wait for another day. Today, he was going to focus on hoping his plan would go the way he wanted.

He looked down the hallway to the exhibit he'd helped set up before turning down the opposite hallway to go meet her. When she turned the corner, he stopped dead in his tracks. She was breathtaking, even in her regular everyday work clothes. Her hair was a little bit tousled from the day, and he wanted nothing more than to grab her cheek in his palm and kiss her. But he resisted, simply because if he did that, she'd be suspicious that something was going on.

Her eyes sparkled when she spotted him, and he couldn't hide the smile that passed across his lips.

"Hey you," she said as she floated down the hall to him.

He embraced her, conscious not to lean in too close to where she'd feel the bulge of the

36

ring in his pocket. Maybe that was overthinking the thing, but he did tend to wear tighter pants than the average man, and the outline of the ring box could be seen in his jeans pocket. He kicked himself inside.

"Where did you want to go to dinner tonight?" she asked.

"I don't know, I was thinking somewhere in the Latin Quarter?" He tried to sound casual. If he said or did anything out of the ordinary, the surprise would be ruined. But why did he want it to be a surprise, anyway? Because that's how people did proposals? Or what—the challenge of it, maybe?

"You ready?" She snapped him out of his thoughts.

He'd hesitated too long. "Uh, yeah. Uhm, really quick, can you show me how far they've gotten on the build of the temporary exhibit?"

She continued walking. "Sure? Why are you so interested? I don't know if they'll let you in without a badge."

"I saw a story about it in the paper and I was just curious. I might... use it for this new book I'm writing, and it'd be neat to see where they're at with it." He'd just thought of that book thing.

"The paper?" She giggled. "Okay, but like I said... they might not let you."

"Never hurts to try!" His voice chirped. *Act natural... act natural.* As they drew closer to his chosen proposal spot, the energy ran rampant through his limbs. He wiped his drenched palms yet again on his pants and slowed his breathing in hopes that Nori wouldn't notice. Amidst the panic, a pleasant swirl of excitement nestled right in-between his rib cage and stomach.

But as he followed behind her, watching her ponytail sway with her hips, he managed to calm himself. *Deep breaths. In and out. You can do this, Parker.*

When they got to the entrance of the exhibit, a man stood in front of the door. He wore navy blue pants and a vest, with a white-collared shirt underneath. A walkie-talkie hung on his hip, and a museum employee lanyard with a badge hung around his neck.

"Salut, Claud..." Nori asked him if it was okay to pass by to see the progress of the exhibit, in French.

Parker smirked behind Nori as he flashed eye contact with Claud, who then avoided his gaze with a slight tug at his lips.

"Pas probleme, Nori." Claud lifted the walkie and spoke quickly into it, then moved out of the way and swung the door open for them. He nodded at Parker as they passed, and Parker mouthed the word *merci* at him.

He reached forward and grabbed Noriana's hand as he caught up to walk next to her, rather than behind her. They were in a dark hallway, with a light that burst from the end. It was bright, brighter than normal, and he looked over to see her brow furrow.

"Hmm, I wonder if they're working on it currently, because this light is never on."

Parker didn't respond, but couldn't contain his smile. As they neared the end of the hallway, he turned to Noriana and stopped her. He grabbed both her hands and turned her towards him.

"Parker..." she breathed, her brow still furrowed.

"Wait," he whispered. "I want to remember this moment right here."

She let out a small, nervous laugh. "What? Why... what's going on?" She asked it as though she knew that he knew what was going on. "Why *this* moment?"

"It's the moment right before our lives change forever," he whispered, then he turned and pulled back the thick, plastic curtain to reveal the banquet room.

He walked in with Nori, who dropped his hand to cover her mouth.

His chest boomed with the pace of his heartbeat. The room was covered in vines, green lacelike vines, from floor to ceiling, with soft accent lighting all pointing towards a painting on the wall. The painting was original. One of a kind. It was Renaissance style, and at first glance, a person might think it was the Coronation of Napoleon painting—the one in Versailles with a replica in the Louvre. His and Nori's shared favorite painting.

Only this one wasn't the queen. It was... Noriana. A painted version of her that caught her likeness. Her beauty glowed. And in front of her in the painting was Parker, on his knees with a shiny object in his hand.

At that moment, Parker fished for the ring in his pocket and then dropped to one knee himself.

Noriana turned to see him after the realization of what was happening sunk into her whole body, displayed by the hands over her mouth and the tears flecking in her eyes.

The light music that played in the background subsided and it felt as though they were in a secret garden together, surrounded by the vines all around them.

"Noriana Taylor Page," he started. "I can't see my life without you. You bring so much enrichment to my life and ..." he choked, catching his breath as his heart beat a million times a second. He had so much more he wanted to say, but he was so nervous his mind was empty. He couldn't conjure the words he'd practiced in his writing. He should have written it down and brought it out to read to her, but he'd wanted to have it memorized. He hadn't envisioned actually freezing up though, and now he wished he had the written version. But he could still give her the paper when they got back home to redeem himself. "... Je t'aime, Noriana. Will you marry me?" His breath rattled, and it felt like ages as his knees began to ache, his fingers trembling with the tiny ring in his hands.

In that moment, the flicker of doubt rang out in his mind. Although there wasn't much room for anything else besides adrenaline, and nerves, and excitement. Of course she could say no. Of course he could feel humiliated by it in front of all their friends and her coworkers, who were waiting just on the other side of those vines to see the outcome of his proposal.

And so he hung on to her every ounce of body language. How she looked around, how she soaked in the painting, and the realization that he was kneeling on the floor. The implications of what that meant. He saw every

41

fiber of her being fill up with emotion and he fed off that, keeping his thoughts positive. It was as though time was speeding and slowing all at the same time.

Tears streamed down Noriana's face and he caught a glimpse of her knees trembling as she knelt down with him on the floor, as though he deserved that. As if he deserved to be at the same level as her.

She cupped his hands with both her own. "Yes! Yes, I'll marry you. Oh my goodness, Parker. I love you."

The words burned into his mind as they floated to his ears. He smiled as he fumbled for her finger and smoothly pushed the ring up onto it. "This was my mother's ring. She wanted you to have it."

"Oh my... it's beautiful." She could barely speak. "You planned... you planned all this?" She looked back over to the painting.

He held her hand. "It wasn't easy with you working here every day."

They both laughed together. Parker rose and pulled Noriana up with him, then embraced her, kissing her soft lips and then spinning her around in the room. Just as he did that, the wall opposite the painting fell from the ceiling to the floor, the vines slinking to the ground, and a crowd erupted in applause and cheering. They both turned to see Noriana's entire museum staff and coworkers clapping and cheering.

Nori put her hand up to cover her mouth again.

Parker put his arm around her shoulders, laughing. He really *did* surprise her. She'd had no idea.

"You all were in on this!" she yelled out in English, however, they all understood her. There was a gentle rattle of laughter from the crowd and some of her closest coworkers zoned in on them, hugging Noriana and grabbing her hand to see her ring displayed.

Parker backed up, his cheeks flushed with excitement and happiness and overwhelm.

Noriana said yes. She was going to be his wife.

He saw Claud approaching and Parker clapped him on the shoulder. "Tres bien, mon ami. Merci beaucoup." He thanked the man for his assistance in the set-up. Parker had been practicing his French.

As the crowd closed in on them to offer congratulations, their support system here in this foreign country that they'd come to call home, he saw nothing but a tunnel to Noriana. The love of his life. The one who had just agreed to spend the rest of her life with him. And yet, it was bittersweet. Because she didn't know what lie just on the other side of tomorrow like he did. The tough conversations they were going to have about how he was going to bring security to their family. And figuring out all the stuff involving the job in Chicago...

But today, he would not allow those thoughts to dampen the happiness he felt right now. Like nothing in the world could change his feelings for her.

Today was for celebration. Celebration of life and love, and the life they could dream for in the future.

FIVE

PARKER

Parker closed the door to their flat and turned around, pressing his back against the door. He watched Noriana remove her coat and place it on the table before bending down to take off her shoes. He followed the curve of her body, across her hips, down her leg.

She looked over her shoulder unexpectedly with a smile across her lips. "Are you checking me out, Mr. Rubec?"

He stifled a small laugh, heat filling his cheeks, but no shame resonated from his heart. "You are so beautiful," was all he could muster from his lips. He only had one thing on his mind and it was the burning desire to feel her up against him with their vulnerability exposed. Of course he wasn't sure how she was feeling and if she was even in the mood tonight. She drove the ship now, and always.

She finished kicking off her shoes and sat on the bed, signaling with her finger for him to come join her.

He floated over, losing his shoes as he went, and moved onto the bed.

"It was fun to celebrate with everyone, but I'm so happy we're alone now," she whispered to him.

He moved in for a kiss.

Her soft lips pressed into his. She moved in deeper and he went with it, mouth to mouth until he retracted for breath. Only for a moment though, before engaging once more. Each connection surged desire through his body.

She pushed off his jacket down to his wrists, holding it there a moment, his wrists restricted behind his lower back. She kissed him down his neck, each peck a small morsel of fire on his skin. He yearned for more. She pulled off the jacket entirely, and he reached for her shirt. He pulled it up, and then stopped, breathing heavy and staring into her eyes.

She nodded, a small smirk upon her lips, and the intimate tension they felt between them was strong. Fierce. He pulled her shirt up and over her head, throwing it to the side. He leaned in and kissed her collarbone, then her neck, then her lips.

She truly was the most beautiful woman he'd ever seen, and he simply could not believe she was his. She'd agreed to marry him. She wore his mother's ring.

His mother. They hadn't even called their families yet to tell them of the news. Of course their families were six hours ahead of them, so they were probably still sleeping—*What in the actual hell? Why am I thinking about my family while my fiancé is ripping off my jeans and smoothing her hand up my leg?*

All thoughts evaporated as her hands wandered over his body, all over his body. He reciprocated, losing himself in the moment and finding himself with her. In the way she breathed, and the noises she made as they moved together as one.

Parker disposed of the condom and cleaned up with a towel before he headed back to the bed. He crawled into the covers. The light under the crack of the bathroom door glowed as Parker heard the toilet flush. It wasn't like the movies. They couldn't just make love and then go to sleep. No. But he lay there, his bare body under the covers, in bliss. It was worth it.

He saw his phone light up on the end table next to the bed, and he rolled over to grab it. It was Stephen. At this hour? His brother did work odd hours as a doctor sometimes, so it wasn't totally out of the ordinary. But why would Stephen be calling him? A slight panic tightened his throat.

He reached out and grabbed the phone. "Hello?"

"Parker! Are you alone?" Stephen's voice presented an urgency that was unwelcome.

Parker's suspicions gripped tighter, but also merited a sinking feeling in his gut. He looked at the bathroom door again and heard the pipes screech from being woken by the shower knobs. He had some time if she was going to take a shower. "Uh, yeah brother. What's up?"

"It's Mom."

A pang of nerves shuddered his chest. "Is she okay? What happened? What's going on?" Parker sat up in the bed.

"She's gone."

Red flags rose everywhere. "What do you mean she's *gone*?" Parker's inflection was accusatory. His stomach churned with panic.

"I—I don't know. She's been gone for more than twenty-four hours. She didn't come home last night and Dad's in a disarray. She doesn't do this."

"Did they have a fight?" Parker turned in the bed and dangled his legs over the side. All bliss of falling asleep calmly had dissipated.

"He says no. He says this is totally out of the blue. Parker, she didn't take her purse or her phone."

An uneasy feeling filled his gut. "Did you call the police?" The obvious question. *Surely, they had.*

"Of course. They said housewives leave all the time. They said they can't do anything unless they find proof that there's been a struggle. They've been questioning Dad as if he's... you know, done something to her."

Parker sighed. "Geezus. He can't take it personally, Stephen. They also have to look to the spouse as the first suspect until he's proven innocent. But that can't be easy. I'll get on the first flight out." He stood from the bed.

"No!"

"What? You expect me to just sit here in another country and not help you guys look for her? What if something really bad happened to her? Stephen, the last time you saw me was not good. I've been... in contact in the last year with some really bad people. What if this is linked?"

Parker heard Stephen let out a rattled breath before he spoke again. "I figured since you survived that, since you're still alive and remaining after the crash of Humavision, that maybe you could help with this. I mean, you haven't told me everything that happened, but it looks like you may have some experience."

Parker warmed. It felt good to have some sort of credibility in the eyes of his successful, doctor brother.

The water pipes seized their ambient humming sound, and suddenly it became eerily quiet in the room. *Noriana. Shit.* Parker had totally forgotten that he needed to discuss the job in Chicago with her, and now this. Of course she'd understand this more than the job thing, but all of it put a damper on their big news. Still, he needed to brush that aside and focus on what really mattered.

Who could have taken Mom? And why? Is it possible she left on her own?

Stephen sighed on the line. "And you're right. I knew by calling you that you'd want to rush home, anyhow." His voice still carried its frantic cadence. "Just… be safe getting here, okay?"

"Yeah, I'll try. Bye." Parker turned off his phone, just as the door to the bathroom opened.

"Who was that?" Nori asked, her eyes still sparkling with the glimmer of her new engagement ring as she rang out her hair with a towel in the doorway, butt-naked.

"Stephen," he choked, his breath taken away by the sight of her.

"Awe, did you call to tell him?" she asked.

Shit. He hadn't even thought to tell his brother he'd just gotten engaged. Maybe it would be better if he fibbed to keep up their façade tonight? No, he couldn't. He couldn't start out his partnership with her by lying. "Actually, no. I wish I'd thought to tell him! He, uhh, had urgent news from back home."

"Oh?"

"I'd rather not talk about it now though, Nori. Let's just go to bed."

"What—C'mon. You can't leave me hanging like that! Is everything okay?"

"No, not exactly. But I don't want to ruin our happiness tonight."

"Parker." She took the towel and wrapped it around her body, snug up underneath her armpits. "I don't want a fairytale with you. I want real life. All of it. The good, the joy, the happiness, and the bad."

"I just wanted to give you one full night to revel in our good news. Call your parents and let them know, just be happy." Parker set his phone on the end table and ran his fingers rigidly through his hair.

Nori walked around and sat on the bed next to him, then turned his face with the touch of her soft hand. The scent of lavender and vanilla wafted from her skin. "If your heart's in a different place right now, so is mine. Tomorrow, we will still be engaged." She raised an eyebrow.

He sighed. She was good. She was too good. She could read him like a book. "It's my Mom." He sensed her inhale sharply, bracing herself for what was coming next. "She's missing."

"What do you mean?"

Parker raised his hands and shrugged. "I don't know. Stephen said they're accusing my Dad and trying to blame him for her being gone. Or trying to tell the family that she left on her own."

"What!? C'mon, they don't know your family." She rubbed the small of his back.

He drooped his head. "I know. He said she didn't take her phone or purse. Something's not right."

"Well you'll have to go there, obviously."

A sense of relief glazed over him. "Do you think I'll be able to help?" It was beginning to sink in. The anxiety of his distance. The fact that his Mom could be in danger. She didn't do this. She'd never leave without letting her sons or husband know where she was going. But then there was also the self-doubt. He looked up at Nori, his eyes suddenly sunk with exhaustion. "But what could I do to help?"

"Hey! Don't do that. Don't put yourself down. You know people from your experiences. You could contact the officer you worked with last year... in Chicago?"

That's when it hit him. The mention of Chicago. The job. It was always a constant nagging in the back of his mind during all of this. "He's in Chicago. How could he help with this?"

"Well Chicago PD could have connections in KC? I don't know." Nori raised her hands.

"It's pretty clear the police aren't helping though..." He sighed. Stephen knew it, too. That's the whole reason he'd reached out to Parker.

Parker tended to have low confidence. To put himself down. To think himself unworthy, or like some loser.

This had to stop. He wasn't a loser. He'd written a best-selling novel. He'd traveled the world. Okay, maybe not the *whole* world, but he'd still taken a chance and traveled out of his comfort zone and thrived. He'd found the woman of his dreams, and she was in love with him, and she'd said yes to marrying him. He might be low on cash right now, but he'd already made a plan to fix that. He was going to secure a job and make a livable wage. He was freakin' living the dream. He was no loser. And he was going to go rescue his mom. Help bring her home. No matter what that entailed. He was going to find out who was at the bottom of this, or if she'd left on her own.

"There is... one more thing." He could gloss over this entirely. He could use the cop-out of his mom going missing to cover-up for the other reason he would have been flying across the pond. But he couldn't do that to Nori. It wasn't right.

"Oh?" she asked, hesitation in her voice.

He was going to go ahead anyway. *Here goes...* "I was offered a job. In Chicago."

"At Humavision," she finished for him.

"You already know?" he asked.

"What other job would be offered to you in Chicago? I knew you couldn't stay away from *him* for very long." She stood from the bed and grabbed a night shirt and shorts from the dresser.

"Ouch?" He felt a little queasy and moved himself to lean against the headboard.

She looked over her shoulder. "Parker, you *just* escaped that nightmare." Nori turned around with the pajamas in her hands. "Why the hell would you go right back into that? Did you... did you already know about this when you asked me to marry you?" She looked down at her hand.

He watched her set the clothes down a moment and spin the ring around with the thumb and index finger of her other hand. His mother's ring. Really, there were more pressing matters than even arguing with his girlfri—fiancé right now. "I need to go to sleep if I'm going to take the first flight out in the morning."

She turned around. "Don't deflect the question, Parker!"

"Yes," he choked out the word. "Okay? Yes! I knew! I was going to tell you tomorrow, after we'd had a night to enjoy our new engagement. After we told our family."

She huffed.

"I'm broke, Nori." He closed his eyes and pinched the bridge of his nose.

"What?"

"I have no more money left. I need a job. My writing isn't selling. Greysen presented a job for me—"

"It could have been *any* other person. Any other job. Let me just take a wild guess... you already accepted the position." She put her hand on her hip. "Without even talking to me about it first."

He looked down into his lap. He was for sure in the dog house. He thought perhaps there was a chance she'd see him as someone who was looking to provide for their family, in any way that he could. That he was making a valiant effort.

Noriana rushed to get dressed, putting her clothes on with a vengeance. Parker looked up to see her wearing jeans and a t-shirt, and she reached for her jacket. Her pajamas were tossed on the floor.

"Where are you going?" Frantic, he stood and reached for her forearm.

She yanked away. "Out."

"It's late, Nori! It's not safe."

"I don't want to spend another second here with you!" She grabbed her phone and keys, then went to the door. "Don't wait up for me."

She slammed the door, hard enough for the walls to rattle. The echo surged through his body, leaving disheveled emotions of loneliness and regret in its wake.

SIX

GREYSEN

Greysen rolled off the couch with his weak muscles and moseyed to the kitchen. With a pounding headache at his temples, he reached for the whiskey that sat on the counter, and then paused, thinking twice about it. *Probably not a good idea...* He pushed the glass bottle to the backsplash and flipped on the faucet, filling his iced cup with water, instead. It'd only been earlier today that he'd had the intense experience with the memory machine, but the effects still resonated through his sore muscles.

The front door slammed around the corner. He startled, turning his head in that direction. Was it his assistant, again? A while back she insisted on having a key to his place and would check in on him periodically. He hesitated, then called out, "Carrie?"

He rounded the corner and stopped dead in his tracks.

A ghost stood in his front foyer.

"Who's Carrie?" Molly's voice was smooth and in control.

He froze. His pulse resonated in his ears. "Molly? What are you..." He had so many questions. He didn't know where to begin. He forgot that his head pounded. The condensing glass in his hand slipped. He set it down on the coffee table and composed his thoughts. "How'd you know where I live now?"

"I've been following you." She stood as still as a board in the foyer.

"Moll, you don't have to do that. Just ask." He raised his arms.

"Moll..." she mocked, laughing under her breath.

"I've always called you that." He thought about the bags under his eyes. The age lines. It was a lifetime ago that he'd been with her. He'd never let her go. He wasn't willing to accept that she'd moved on.

They continued to stand there, each holding their ground, still. He'd nearly forgotten that his body was weak and unstable.

He hadn't seen her since they'd left that motel room. He wasn't sure where she'd gone, only that she wasn't interested in continuing her relationship with him, even as friends. He understood she wanted and needed to move on then, even if he didn't want to accept it.

"Why are you here?" he asked.

"The memory chip," she said softly.

She couldn't possibly know he'd seen memories with her in them. She'd been so upset in that motel room. She'd made him promise not to watch them. But she knew he still had them in his possession. Maybe that was what was bothering her? He didn't respond. He waited for her to elaborate.

"I'm here to warn you."

His heart sank. "About what?" It could be a number of things.

"I know you still have it. And I know you've been sifting through the memories."

"How—"

"Don't ask me how I know, Greysen."

The sound of his name on her tongue gave him pause. A warm feeling in his gut. He pushed the thoughts aside. Even after twenty years she had a hold on him.

She continued, "He's manipulating you. Even in death."

Greysen narrowed his eyes.

"You can't believe what you see."

He wanted to move closer to her, but was afraid he'd scare her off. "But they're memories, Molly. He can't fake a *memory*. They were siphoned directly from his mind. The memory device doesn't lie."

She shook her head, clearly showing her frustration. She glanced down at her phone. Why was she so worried about the time? Worried about visiting him at all?

"Listen carefully, okay? You are viewing those memories as Edrick lived them. As he *remembers* them. You're seeing those scenes as he *perceived* them, not as they actually happened. Why would you trust his memories, if you could *never* trust him living?"

The words burned into his mind as he realized the truth of them. *Damn.*

"There is... one more thing." With her head tilted toward the ground, she looked up at him.

His stomach tightened.

"There was... an invention you'd been working on. A while back. Like, before all this." She paused to take a breath, but kept her eyes trained on him. "The one I helped you with?"

He nodded. He knew the very specific one she spoke of. Not the memory machine. Not even the DDT. This was one they'd worked on together back in the olden days.

60

"Greysen, we both used our DNA during the research for that one... and I searched high and low for the prototype when you fled the country. I couldn't find it anywhere. The rest of the equipment was destroyed but they had back up servers. We both know this. That infor—"

"I can assure you Molly, it is safe." He stabilized himself against the doorframe to the kitchen. "Please, come in for a moment. We can sit in the family room and catch up."

Her brow furrowed.

"But... I can't tell you what I did with the prototype. It's safe. I put it on a computer chip and sent it away to a safe location, where it will never be found." The swirling in his gut made him feel ill. He didn't even believe the words himself once they left his mouth. Surely, she'd catch onto that.

She took one long look at him. "I have to go." She turned to the door.

"Wait!" He reached out for her, though he knew he was too far away to actually touch. "Are you okay? I mean... are you safe?"

She laughed under her breath again. "You don't need to worry about me. Are *you*?"

Valid question. One he didn't know the answer to. *Does she?* "I mean, can you tell me you're not involved in any of this stuff anymore?

Since you... disappeared. Please tell me you've started over somewhere. You're no longer in this mess?" He wasn't actually sure if the death of Edrick was the end of the toxic power involved in Humavision. He was unaware of her working for the company anymore after that day in the motel, so he'd assumed she'd gotten away. He'd hoped she did. But he also didn't know if that was possible.

She looked down at her phone again, then up at him, and gave a shrug.

He felt a chill across his shoulders. It was out of character for her. Did he even know her character anymore?

She turned to leave.

"Molly?"

She stopped for a moment with her hand on the doorknob.

"Can you tell me one thing?" He wasn't even entirely sure she would know this answer. The fact she didn't move told him to continue before it was too late. "In one of the memories..."

She audibly sighed.

"... Edrick reached out to Dottie. I just need to know that she's safe. That she's untouched."

From Molly's profile, he saw her lip curve upward. "You've always hung onto her, huh?"

He didn't know how to answer that.

"Greysen, you need to let go. You can't save everyone."

He fired up inside. "You didn't answer me." He began to question everything about her presence here. *What is she getting at?* She most definitely was not the same Molly he'd left when he'd fled Chicago the first time. That Molly was gone. He knew nothing about this woman full of secrets. And he wondered what side she was really on. Was the fact she was here an indication? Or did that just confuse things even more? Did she know the pull she still had on him?

"You didn't answer my question," he repeated sternly.

"I don't know." She stared him straight in the eyes. "I can't help you with that."

So this is how things are going to be? He nodded. Her answer both relieved and concerned him. But it was worth a try.

"Get a better door lock. So people can't just walk in here," she said, and with that, pulled the door closed behind her.

Greysen turned on his side, groaning. His head pounded, and it seemed as though the light was just too bright in the room. He squinted. Just when he tried to push himself to a seated position on the bed, the palm of a hand came down on his forehead and pushed him back against the pillow.

"Oh *no* you don't." Her voice was stern.

"Carrie, where am—" He recognized her voice before he saw her. She was knelt down rummaging through a bag she must have brought with her.

It was his assistant, Carrie. "You're at home, Mr. Price."

"Please, how many times have I told you to—" His throat scratched every time he spoke. He put his hand to his Adam's apple. "—to cut the formality. Greysen is fine."

"Slow down there, old man." She stood and spun around to him, something in her hand. "First, take this aspirin. Then, wash it down with this." She shoved the glass into his hand and cranked his neck forward. "A concoction to raise your electrolytes."

"God! Why are you being so..." The aspirin knocked the back of his throat and he choked it down with the water.

"Because I'm pissed. You could have killed yourself. You promised you wouldn't go under without supervision." She grabbed the glass from his hand and clunked it on the end table.

"Did I... promise?" He smirked.

She did not return the sentiment. "You know I've been slaving over that prototype. It needs a lot of work. It shouldn't be operating right now. And you shouldn't be working, either. You need to rest. Recover." She packed her bag back up.

"Carrie, please. I can explain. You have to understand that I'm searching for something. It's important."

She turned to his bed and knelt at his side.

He saw the genuine kindness in her eyes. She'd bothered enough to be upset with him. She'd checked up on him, most likely in confidence. She was a good employee. A good friend.

"Look, *Greysen*." She emphasized the use of his name. "You're a good boss and a kind man. But I have two things to say to you. First, don't let yourself get lost in your own creation. Second, I do not want to be involved in your personal vendetta. I'm here to do a job and cash a paycheck. I'm very passionate about my job, yes, but I want to know very little about why you're nearly killing yourself surfing through other people's memories—which, by the way, is not what your invention was intended for, I remind you. Just let me do my job and go home for the day with clean hands, is that too much to ask?" She stood and threw the bag over her shoulder.

He'd heard *most* of that. He faded in and out of consciousness. *So tired…* Of course, he didn't want to involve her, either. She was a smart collaborator, with medical experience to boot, and had a drive like none he'd ever come across in his line of work. He needed her on his side. But she was right, he didn't need to bring her down this path of vindication. "It's not too much to ask. Thank you, for all you've done and continue to do... for this company, Carrie. And for me." He rested his head back.

She walked to the door of his bedroom. "Just, please get rest, okay? Before you act on anything you may or may not have experienced these past twenty-four hours." She went for the door. "I'll let myself out."

He turned from his side back to flat and grunted a "thank you" in her direction as the door closed.

Since his return, he'd been renting a small, one-bedroom apartment. All those years ago, before Paris, he'd abandoned his townhouse and everything inside, allowing it to be foreclosed on. That was a given, and he'd known that's what would happen when he'd left it.

Had he lived the life he'd strived for? When he looked back on it now, was it everything he'd wanted it to be? He was alone, in a small apartment. He'd risked everything for his job, then had no choice but to walk away from it, and now he had his dream job. But at what cost?

At the cost of feeling as though someone was constantly breathing down his neck? Constantly looking over his shoulder? Losing everyone he loved, and not being able to settle down? No wife. No family. What were the things that were most important to him?

And even now, Was the simple fact he was trying to figure out who ran Edrick even worth it? He'd longed and longed for that villain to be gone, and now that he was, what was left?

SEVEN

PARKER

Parker woke up the next morning with a splitting headache. He turned and scanned the bed next to him with blurry vision. It was empty, and the sheets were cold when he grazed his hand across them. *Noriana never came home last night.* A sinking feeling settled in the pit of his stomach and he pushed himself up, his legs hanging off the side of the bed. He touched the ground, though felt far from grounded. He pressed his palms into his eye sockets.

Was it all over before it even began? Last night, he'd asked Noriana, the girl of his dreams, to marry him. And she'd said yes. But now... this? Regardless, he had an obligation. He was going to have to push aside his feelings, because in the greater scheme of things, his mother was in danger. He checked his phone and saw he had a text come in from Stephen.

His heart flipped. Perhaps it was a message saying they'd found her, and everything was okay, that she had just wandered off. Instead it read, "What's your flight time? I'll come get you."

So this was still on.

He switched apps on his phone to the airline app and retrieved the information, then pasted it back on the conversation with Stephen. "I should be there in a day or so, with connection in Chicago."

He got up. He shook from the morning chill in the air of the apartment and started to dress. Then, he pulled a duffle bag out from under the bed and threw some clothes into it. It didn't even matter what.

He looked around the apartment, cold and lonely. He needed to get going, he couldn't stall any longer. But Nori wasn't back yet, if she was even going to come back. He wanted to say goodbye. He pulled out his phone again and called her. Straight to voicemail.

Parker sighed, then pulled out a piece of paper and wrote a note:

Noriana, I'm sorry. For everything.

Then he signed his name in chicken scratch, left it on the kitchen counter with a print-out of his flight itinerary, and went out the door.

Charles De Gaulle airport was hustling and bustling, as usual. He was very familiar with this airport, having done this trip so many times before. And this wasn't the first time he'd taken the trip with a longing in his soul. Each and every time he had something pull him from one end of the pond to the other, both ways.

Exiting the RER train into the crowd of people, he moved towards the TSA line. At the stanchions, he put his duffle bag down and reached in his back pocket for his passport.

"Parker."

His head shot up and the passport dropped to the ground.

Noriana stood there, wearing a jacket and a beanie on her head. She dropped her suitcase on the ground and shrugged.

He blinked. *Am I imagining this?* The moment passed quickly, and the questions sunk in. *Suitcase.* "What... what are you doing?" He reached down and scooped up his passport and duffle. A family was moving in on him. "Oh desole," he said sorry in French to them. "Excusez-moi." He moved aside and motioned for them to go in front of him, then grabbed his duffle and moved quickly to Noriana.

He dropped his bag again and threw his arms around her, pressing his nose into her hair. Lavender. Honey. "You didn't come home. I didn't think I'd see you before I left."

She pressed her hands on the small of his back.

"Nori—" he pushed back again. "You can't come with me," he said it reluctantly.

"You have no choice. I'm coming. Parker, we're a team."

He couldn't help the corner of his lips from twitching into a smile. "What made you decide to come?"

She held up her arm, the back of her hand facing Parker. The sparkle on her ring finger caught his eye, and with that, a lump in his throat.

"She's my family too. If you go —" She put her hand on his chest, then retracted it. "—I go."

He shook his head. "It could be dangerous."

"At this point... I feel like that's our life motto." She smiled and moved a piece of her hair behind her ear.

He chuckled under his breath.

"And I want to support you in any way I can."

He leaned into her. "Well how can I deny that?" he whispered softly into her ear. He kissed her, all the hustle and bustle of the airport melting away around them.

Parker looked down at her ring again. She'd kept it on, regardless of their fight.

"But—" Nori began as she pulled away. "You're not off the hook about this copywriting job. You went behind my back, and that's not cool." She crossed her arms.

Parker looked down at his shoes. The words although spoken softly, struck like a scolding. "I deserve that. It wasn't cool. I was trying to secure a way to support us without it seeming like I couldn't do it on my own."

She stared a moment, her eyes half closed as though she was not amused. "You're just so clueless sometimes." She sighed.

Guilt ripped his insides. He really didn't mean to piss her off. But she was here, now, and they had more pressing matters to get to. He would make it up to her. "Okay, you're coming with me." He grabbed her hand and headed for the line to get through security.

He had no clue what lay ahead. Fear, worry, anxiety, paranoia, determination, hope... and now, he had a partner with him to do it all.

He stood next to Nori with his bag in his hand, staring at the departure monitors. The lines of flights blurred together in his vision.

"It's been canceled!"

His heart sank. "What? Canceled?"

"Yes, look!" She pointed up at the monitor, which switched screens before he saw it.

His head was hot and he rubbed his eyes. "Well now what're we going to do?" His voice sounded hoarse.

"We can go to our gate and see what happened. And try to get on another connection. Hey, it'll be okay." Her face wore a look of concern.

He nodded and followed after her. People rushed around him as the two of them pushed against the traffic of travelers.

When they got to the gate, Nori joined the group of frazzled people waiting in line at the desk. Parker pulled out his phone and found a quiet corner. He dialed his brother's number, then leaned against a pole.

"Stephen, our flight's been canceled." His voice was frantic.

"Canceled? You looking for another flight?"

Parker glanced over his shoulder at the desk. "Nori's trying to get us another one. But it's going to delay us getting home. How are things there?"

"The same really. Don't worry, Parker. We're doing all that we can here. You'll get here when you get here, okay man? Some things are out of our control."

He sighed. Stephen was right. That still didn't make his anxiety go away. "I'll keep you updated okay?"

"Look on the bright side. Chicago is where you have your connections, right? If you're stuck there... "

The thought *had* crossed his mind. In fact, he'd thought of the possibility of his mom missing having something to do with his involvement in *The Idea Man,* for the entirety of the flight getting here. "Good idea, man. If we can't get out of here tonight, I'll see if I can drum up some help here." He looked up to see Nori coming back over to him. Her face looked grim. "Gotta go. I'll update you!" They hung up just as she made her way back.

"Not good. No other flights out of here until the AM."

Parker dropped his arms to his sides. "Nothing?"

"We can rent a car?" She tensed her

shoulders. "They're offering to put us up in a hotel overnight."

"I talked to Stephen. He says they're doing what they can there, so... He also mentioned maybe I should talk to my connections while stuck here."

"There's an idea. You have to set-up base for your job as well. Maybe you just reach out to Greysen on both accounts?"

Parker nodded. "Let's get outta here." He stretched his neck back and forth. Perhaps it would be a good idea to get his job established and have a conversation with Greysen. He had to know whether or not his mom's disappearance had anything to do with his involvement with Greysen, and the dangerous people that seemed to follow him wherever he went.

It was mid-afternoon when they took a rideshare to a cheap motel and brought their bags to the room.

"We won't be here long," he told Noriana as he watched her scan the paisley bedspread with that look on her face.

"No, it's... okay!" Her voice was higher-pitched than normal.

Parker smiled. She didn't want to be rude or sound snobby. Because she wasn't. "If you want, I can get my blacklight out of the bag?" he joked.

She gave him one of those looks that said 'stop' but with a sly smile. "I think I'd rather not," she exclaimed, even though he knew she knew he didn't actually possess a blacklight. "I just don't understand why we didn't take the airline up on their offer for the hotel close to there."

"I told you, this crap motel is closest to the business district downtown. I can walk to Humavision and back." Parker grabbed his messenger bag and threw open the top to make sure he had everything he needed inside.

She nodded, then walked over to the bathroom and peeked in the door.

"I want to spend as little time here as possible, so I can get to my family. I think I'll walk over to Humavision now and get it over with. When I called Greysen at the airport, he said he rescheduled a meeting so he could meet with me."

Nori looked over her shoulder at him. "That's nice of him. How far away is KC from here?"

He sighed. "Three-hour plane ride. It'd be too long to drive."

"Is there anything I can do to help while you're gone?" she asked, coming back out into the main room.

"You are so sweet. I'll text you if something comes up." And with that, he kissed her and then went to the door. "I'll make sure to tell the guy at the check-in counter that we'd like to book this place for our honeymoon." He winked at Noriana and closed the door before he could catch her reaction.

As he walked down the pavement, his smile faded. It wasn't called the Windy City for nothing. The wind whipped his balance every which way. He felt the exhaustion coat over him as if an egg had been cracked on his head, trickling down. He'd been able to get an hour or so of sleep on the flight over, but not nearly enough. It was always as if traveling was so exhausting, even though he did nothing but sit there. And the night before, he hadn't gotten a good sleep either because of his fight with Nori.

He still hadn't asked her where she'd gone that night. Since she hadn't mentioned it, he didn't think it was a big deal and he was willing to let it go for the simple fact that she wasn't mad anymore at all the stupid stuff he did.

He waited at a crosswalk for the light to turn red. A truck flew by on the road, filling the air with exhaust. He shoved his face into his arm.

He still wasn't so sure about the idea of working for Humavision. But it was something he felt compelled to do. He needed to make a living. He needed to show something for himself. But was doing that with *this* company really the right answer? This would definitely take him away from their life in Paris, which was something he knew Noriana would not give up—and he didn't want her to. Would they really do a long-distance relationship? Again?

He wasn't sure if he was made for that. And because he'd asked her to marry him now, that wasn't even an option anymore. Perhaps today he could get Greysen to agree to allow him to work remotely, fly-in for a few meetings here and there.

His thoughts were enough to take him the length of the walk, and he zeroed in on the Humavision building.

He took a deep breath and harnessed any ounce of courage he had inside.

After he walked through the building's security, he was approached by a young, studious woman. "Hello, can I help you?"

"Yes, hi. Uh, my name is Parker Rubec, I'm meeting with Greysen Price this afternoon?" He posed it as more of a question than anything. "About a new job?"

She looked down at her phone. "Parker. Yes, I have you on his schedule here. I'm Carrie. I'm Mr. Price's assistant."

He reached out and shook her hand. "Carrie? Hi." *Assistant? Of Greysen's? And one that calls him Mr. Price, at that. This'll be weird to get used to.*

"This way."

He followed behind her, tripping over his feet to catch up. She wound him through hallways, up an elevator, and to a floor with a long hallway of doors. He followed her to a room that had floor-to-ceiling windows. A conference room with a large table and chairs all around. A man stood at a window overlooking the city. They were high enough to where they couldn't be seen from down below though.

Carrie moved into the room through the open door. "Sir?"

The man in the suit spun around, and Parker was floored. "Greysen? Haha!" He dropped his messenger bag on the table and went to the man, slapping his arms around him in a hug. "You clean up, man!"

Greysen laughed. "Good to see you, Parker. Thanks, Carrie." He nodded to her.

Carrie turned to leave. "I'll let you guys get reacquainted, and then I'll show Parker to his office."

"My office?" Parker looked from Carrie and back to Greysen. He wasn't sure if he should be happy or not. "I really don't need—"

"While you're here, it's your home. We'll treat you well."

Parker was still trying to get used to the sight of a clean-shaven, well-manicured Greysen. "Well, I appreciate it."

"Carrie, I can show him there, no need to stick around. I know you've got a lot to do."

She nodded, "Okay, well thanks. I'm glad you made it here safely, Parker. I'll see you around." Carrie spun on her heels and left.

"How are ya, man?" Parker asked.

Greysen leaned on the table with both hands. "I'm good. Yeah, I'm good. I'm glad you called me. Glad you finally decided to take this copywriting job. We can pay you well, and you are a talented writer."

Parker hesitated. "Well we should talk about specifics of the job first, really. Hammer out if it's possible for me to work remotely before you close applications for this job. But yeah, it's...

81

weird to be back here." His gaze arched to the ceiling, and around the conference room. He'd never been in this particular space before, but the odd feeling extended to the whole of the building itself. "You know, with all that shit that happened last year."

"I know what you mean." Greysen returned the sentiment. "So much history has happened here for me. But I can't let that stop me from moving forward, you know?"

Parker nodded.

"This room in particular... this is where I pitched my invention for the Disease Detection Technology."

Parker saw the scene unfold before him in his mind. Where Greysen had stood in that same room all those years ago, nervous but hopeful. He shared something with Greysen that nobody else could. He knew Greysen's whole history from Greysen's perspective. He watched the man ponder his own thoughts.

Parker faced the large windows, the dull aching thought of his mom's disappearance suddenly taking precedence over anything else. Guilt crept into his conscience for the simple fact that he thought about something else for a moment. He wasn't sure if he should drop his troubles on Greysen just yet or not. Perhaps he shouldn't involve the man at all. Since they'd just got back in contact, he didn't want Greysen thinking he was there to take advantage of his resources, or that he was only there for help and not to work the job. But, that was the entire reason *why* he was there, after all.

However, in the moment, even though it was burning inside and pulling and pulling at him, he decided he wasn't going to bring up the issues with his family right away. He'd establish his role here, first. Not to mention, after the shock of a Greysen who was groomed, Parker could see right through him. The man seemed stressed. His sunken eyes looked like he hadn't slept in days, more tired than jetlagged Parker himself even looked.

Greysen scratched the back of his head and looked away from Parker's gaze. "Well, let me show you your home base. If you just got in this morning, I imagine you're exhausted from the flight."

"Yeah, that'd be great," Parker reciprocated. He followed behind Greysen as they exited the conference room and headed down the hall.

"To your right is my office, in case you need to get a hold of me for anything. But your office is riiiight—" They turned a corner. "Here." He opened a door and ushered Parker inside.

It was cozy. A desk and a nice window. Nothing too special. It was nice for them to offer him a space, but he also felt quite isolated in an office like this. The pay was good, but honestly, that alone wasn't really worth it for him. The office life might be okay for Greysen, but he was a free bird. Also, he'd hoped he'd spend no time in here anyway, since he wanted to secure a position remotely. That was the whole point of taking the job offer.

A weary feeling washed over him entirely. *Is this for sure what I wanted? Is it too late to back out? Why is money the root of all decisions? Ugh.* "Thanks, man. I'll get situated here. We should do dinner or something. I have Noriana here. Plus, I have some stuff to ask you..."

"Oh yeah? Nori came with you!?"

"I couldn't make her stay back." Parker smiled. "I've asked her to marry me. And for some reason, she said yes."

"Parker! Congratulations, oh my god!" Greysen raised his arms.

"I'm really excited." Parker angled his face away from Greysen, but he couldn't hide his widening smile.

"I am... Parker, I am so proud of you." Greysen clapped his hand on Parker's shoulder.

Parker looked into Greysen's face. He was being genuine.

"You are the closest I have to any kind of family. I'm happy you are here. I need to get back to work, but I wanted you to know that."

Parker felt a twinge when Greysen said that, bogged down by the fact he hadn't told Greysen about the true and main reason why he'd come here. He couldn't just yet. However, on the other side of that feeling was an elated happiness. He hadn't told anyone in his family yet about the engagement because of what had happened immediately afterwards. And sharing the news about it gave him an unexplainable pride and joy.

"You can hit me up later about where you want to meet for dinner, okay?" Greysen finished, then left the room.

Parker stood in his new office and turned around. It was small, yes, but at least he had a nice window. He thought briefly of the possibilities of how he could decorate it. Posters on the walls. Perhaps his Death Star lamp on the desk. Would he be one of those guys who had a photo of his fiancé?

"Screw that..." he breathed. He wasn't going to be here. He wouldn't stay here. He'd be working remotely. Not stuck in this office in Chicago. No. He was *not* an office guy.

He moved around to the desk and pulled back the rolling chair. The office was furnished with a nice, modern computer. It beat his laptop, that was for sure. Immediately he regretted thinking ill of his laptop. He'd written the novel that had made him eight hundred thousand dollars on that laptop. He sat down and took out his cell phone. The service was good here.

Parker looked up at the closed door. He heard muffled voices rushing down the hall, which meant that whenever he spoke inside his office, nobody could hear his conversation outside the door. His voice would also be muffled.

He quickly texted Nori, "Settled in. G was happy to see me. You okay there?" Then, before she responded, he called his brother.

"Parker." Stephen sounded exasperated.

"Hey, I'm in Chicago, any news?"

"Nothing, man. I'm getting restless. Dad's losing his shit."

"What are the police saying?" He rested his chin on his hand and pressed the phone harder into his ear.

"Along the same lines as before. They're saying they don't put amber alerts out on adults. We can file a missing person's report, but we don't have much information on what she was wearing when she went missing. We gave a photo, though. They're asking incriminating questions of the whole family, saying most of the time bored housewives just take off."

"Screw them," Parker interjected.

"No, I know. They're saying if she was taken, it's most likely someone she knew because there was no sign of a struggle, anywhere. They say it's a pretty high statistic of it usually being the husband."

"To hell with statistics!" Parker stood, and the chair rolled back and hit the wall. "Stephen. We know that Dad didn't and wouldn't do anything to hurt her."

"I know, man. But still. It's just tough on everyone. Where is she? Nothing like this has ever happened before, you know? Something's up."

Parker rubbed his eye with his free hand. "Well I'll be home soon. In the meantime, at my pitstop in Chicago, I'm working on talking to someone who I think can help us."

"I thought about reaching out to a Private Investigator too," Stephen said. "I don't think it's too early to do that if the police aren't going to move their asses on this."

Parker hesitated a moment. "That's not a bad idea. But let me talk with my connection first."

"Can I ask you how you came across this connection? Parker, you've never told me about anything that happened last year when I came and visited you in Chicago. When you had that... head injury." His concerned tone softened his voice.

"I know, Stephen. There's things about me—" Parker stifled a laugh, "—that you wouldn't believe."

"Would any of those things... now this is just an inkling. Don't get mad. But would any of what happened to you have anything to do with Mom going missing?"

Wow. It's like his brother pulled the thoughts right out of his head. But really, what could the connection possibly be? *There's no way.* What had happened to him ended once Greysen assumed ownership of Humavision. The threat was gone. The memory machine was under wraps. Nobody would be out to get him or his family. He'd lived peacefully for quite some time in Paris with Noriana after the end of that crazy shit, and nothing had followed him there. This couldn't be related.

"Parker?"

His attention teetered back to the phone. "No. I don't think so, Stephen. What happened to me last year is in no way related." *I hope.* He closed his eyes and pinched the bridge of his nose with his free hand.

"So you're not going to tell me, then?"

He sighed, leaning back against the wall. "Not in a phone call, brother. Please understand. When you came to help me out in that motel all that time ago, you said you weren't going to ask questions or pry into what was going on, that you'd just fix me up and be on your way. That is why we're talking now. I haven't even heard from Marshall. We don't have the relationship like you and I do. Just, please continue to give me that respect." He wiggled the mouse and glanced at the time on the computer monitor. "And anyway, let me do my thing here. And then I will reach back out to you to contact that PI. I plan to be in KC tomorrow morning on the first flight I can get. I hope that's not too late."

"I'll do all I can here. I'll wait for your call."

"Thanks, man," Parker finished. "Bye."

They hung up.

He looked down at the phone after hitting *end*. Noriana's reply text came through, "I'm fine here. Hurry back."

He texted, "Dinner with G?" Then he sat back in the chair and thought about Stephen's call. Really, he couldn't pinpoint anything that might connect him and his involvement with Humavision being the reason for his mom's kidnapping after thinking about it for so long. *We're just going to call it a kidnap. Let's be real. She did not just take off. She would never do that willingly.* A reply text interrupted his thoughts.

"Georgio's Italian. 7pm."

She was always so good at making plans and decisions. Way better than he was. He responded, "I'll let him know."

EIGHT

PARKER

Parker pulled up his email on the computer. Did they fully expect him to work right now? In this office? He felt so disjointed. Why did Greysen leave him here so quickly? The whole reason he came to Humavision today was to talk with him and establish his position, as well as ask about his mom. Nori and him weren't even supposed to be spending this much time in Chicago in the first place.

Mom.

Where could she be?

Is she safe?

Is she scared?

Will we ever find her?

How's Dad coping? Stephen had said he wasn't doing well.

How would I feel if something like this happened to Noriana?

He'd fight tooth and nail for her return. He'd never believe she'd left him for another man. Or for another life.

And his mom hadn't either. *Someone took her.* And if the police were not going to help them, then they'd have to figure it out themselves. He'd gotten out of bad situations before, and he was going to do that now. His family had no idea what he'd been through in the last year or so.

But there was one person, besides Nori, who *did* know what had happened. There was one person who was the cause of all his hardships and his triumphs: Greysen Price. And now Parker was right back in that man's web again, sitting in this building, in this office. Was this all a mistake?

He opened a few emails, one telling him about a meeting he'd need to be at next week. *Great.* He already had projects. He'd already have to be in Chicago for his job next week. Perhaps there would be a lot of that in the beginning, and then he could work remotely?

He opened one email from Carrie. *Who's Carrie, again? Oh yeah, Greysen's assistant.* It outlined some of the points of the first marketing campaign he needed to launch.

Writing fiction was one thing. And of course he'd had experience writing non-fiction too, although it had been disguised as fiction. Writing 'copy' was a whole other world.

But he could do it.

He would do it.

For his new family.

For the paycheck.

He was lucky to be able to work a job in the field he desired. He'd come a long way from the beginning when he was living back in Kansas City before everything began.

He had a feeling he'd be getting really comfortable with having Carrie in his life, having to work hand-in-hand with her. She seemed nice enough to get along with. And if Greysen trusted her, she must be all right.

He pushed back in his chair. Greysen had said he needed to get back to work, but Parker thought he'd go down to his office and pop his head in, briefly let him know what they'd decided on for dinner. Or, perhaps he could also have that sensitive conversation with him too, instead of tonight at dinner. And perhaps he could ask why Greysen looked so exhausted and worn. He'd avoided the topic earlier. They'd just reunited, and he didn't want to insult the man right off the bat. He had no clue the kind of work Greysen had to deal with being the CEO of this company. Maybe it wasn't all what it was chalked up to be. Maybe he was in over his head, biting off more than he could chew.

And Parker was aware in the end all, Greysen was an inventor. Perhaps that was eating away at him, too. Perhaps Greysen had learned that when running the company, he had to put aside being the technician. Maybe that weighed heavy on him.

But what weighed heavy on Parker was the fact his mom had been missing for too long now. And he needed to pull his resources together. Greysen knew powerful people. Greysen had been willing to go out on a limb for Parker time after time.

He needed to at least try to enlist the man's help in this situation, as well.

Parker walked down the hallway, listening carefully to all the voices as he passed rooms. Though nothing really came into focus. And none of them were voices he recognized. He kept going, in the direction Greysen had told him his office was.

As he neared the door, he heard Greysen's voice and his stomach flipped. He flexed his fists, the damp palms evident. *Why am I so nervous?*

Greyson straight up just told me I was like family to him.

He just didn't want Greysen thinking he was taking advantage after everything he'd done for him.

He was about to push on the door and peek his head inside when something in Greysen's voice caught his attention and froze him in mid-motion. It was the frantic tone that caught him off guard.

"JUST TELL ME."

At first, he thought the person Greysen yelled at was also in the office. But when the conversation was not reciprocated, he knew Greysen must have been talking on the phone.

"Why did you follow me and look me up if you weren't there to give me information?"

Parker grappled with the idea of knocking or leaving. *Maybe I should turn around. This is none of my business.* He shook his head. *I can just ask him at dinner tonight, no big deal. Or...you know, I could just email him!*

And then he heard it.

"I saw the memory with Dottie in it. They reached out to her. I know it."

Every muscle in his body tensed. Why was his mother's name just spoken on Greysen's lips? Did he know her? *There's no way!* There were other

Dottie's in this world. But no. It was too relevant. His whole world began to crumble as Stephen's voice resonated in his head. Perhaps there *was* a connection. A connection he knew nothing about. How could he? How could he be so naive?

He couldn't go into that office. Nothing made sense. He pricked his ears and leaned closer to the door, trying to hear more.

"Why would I see that in Edrick's memories then, huh? When I fled, they had to cover all their bases... But I was for sure they'd never find out about her."

Find out about her? Find out what? Does Mom know Greysen or something?

Regardless, Parker was in a fit of rage. He turned to march back to his office when he collided with someone in the hall, smashing into the hardness of their skull. He fell backwards into the wall, clutching his forehead as he gasped. "I'm so sorry... I didn't—"

He looked up to see Carrie rubbing her own head, a perplexed look on her face. "Whatareya doing?" she slurred.

"Uh." He hesitated. His headache from this morning was back. He most likely would have a huge goose egg emerge later. Parker tried to be quiet for a moment to see if he heard Greysen talking anymore, but it was silent. Greysen must have heard their collision. He needed to get out of there before Greysen came out of his office.

Too late.

The office door opened and Greysen stood there, looking at the both of them in bewilderment. "Carrie? Parker? What's, uhh—"

Parker lifted his hands in surrender. "Nothing! No one! I mean... "

Carrie laughed, looking at Parker as if he had an eye on his forehead. "You're acting so strange."

"I'm just jostled, is all. I came to tell you—" He pointed at Greysen, trying to level his voice, "—that I'm sorry, but Nori and I can't do dinner. We'll have to take a raincheck." He could barely look him in the eye. "Just shaken from crashing into you." He nodded at Carrie. "You okay? I should have been paying attention."

She laughed, her eyebrow cocked. "I'm good."

"Great. See you then." He pushed past her in a hurry, not making eye contact with either of them.

"Parker!" Greyson called out.

He tensed. *Shit.* He looked over his shoulder. "Ya?"

"You didn't ... uh, hear anything from the phone call I was just on, did you?" His voice was more incriminating than anything.

"Phone call? No, didn't realize you were on the phone. Should I have?"

"No, no you're good." Greyson looked down and shook his head. Then headed back for his office.

Carrie stood between them, looking from one to the other.

"You coming?" Greysen barked at Carrie.

She peeped and jumped, following him into the office and shutting the door.

Parker took off down the hall as fast as his feet could drag him. He needed to stop at his office and grab his stuff. And he needed to get out of there.

Fast.

The words of Greysen's phone call buzzed in his head.

NINE

PARKER

P arker used his key card in the door and burst into the motel room. He threw his bag on the small round table by the window and rushed for his duffle, stuffing the things he'd just previously pulled out not too long ago back into it.

Noriana sat on the bed, bracing herself on both sides with her hands. "Parker, what in the hel—"

He sat on the edge of the bed and shoved a shirt into the bag. "Pack your things. We're going. No dinner."

"What happened?" she pressed on.

He felt the weight of her moving off the bed. She came over to his side and placed her hand over his on the strap of the duffle bag. Parker tried all he could to not allow the emotion to play over his face, but he was fuming. First with

99

anger, and then an overwhelming sadness overcame him. His eyes welled up uncontrollably.

"Parker?" She tossed her arms around him and he pulled close into her body. It was a good thing she'd come on this trip. If she wasn't here, he might have done something irrational by now. He breathed into her shoulder a moment, letting his emotions sink in. He needed a level head. He needed to bring himself back to the present and put his thinking cap on. There was a solution to this. "Greyson must be involved," he said finally. "With my mom going missing. I heard him talking on the phone with someone. I'm not sure who. But he mentioned my mom's name."

She just listened. She didn't try and talk him out of his reasoning or rationalization. She just let him explain to her all that he'd heard. He continued, knelt down by the bed, and when he'd finished, she spoke up. "What are we going to do now?"

"We're going." He stood up and shook off her hold on his arm. "I'm not staying here. We have to get to Kansas City. Stephen's hiring a PI."

"A PI?" She sounded impressed. "Parker, you can't leave just yet," she suggested.

"Why? I can't trust him."

She matched him in standing. "Whoa, whoa. I wouldn't jump to that conclusion just yet."

"Nori, he's hiding something and I—"

"But you have to consider everything you two have been through, Parker. I'm not trying to defend Greysen by any means, but I want you to think rationally here. He could still be a big help in finding your mom. And... well he doesn't know you heard him, right?" She coaxed him back onto the bed.

Parker sat down. "I don't... think so. I mean I reacted like an idiot when I was caught outside his door, but I don't think he knows I heard."

"Well then that's just it. You can't let him know that you know. You still have an inside with Greysen. You have access to everything in that building, yes? Perhaps there's something in there that can help us find your mom. And... and if you leave right now, he'll suspect something is up, right? We *just* got here." She slowly reached out to take the duffle bag from him.

He looked down at the duffle, surrendering it to her. "And what about me asking for his help and using his resources?"

"Well, now, we just established that we aren't sure whether we can trust him, or not."

Parker nodded.

101

"So take him for what it's worth." She tugged at his shoulder and he hugged her once more.

He wiped his eyes from their residual blurriness. "I just can't do dinner with him tonight as planned. I'll blow my cover. I'm too angry."

She nodded. "That's okay, we'll figure something else out. It's your lunch break now? Or are you done for the day?"

Shit. Parker had forgotten that the normal work day wasn't finished yet. For one, all he'd wanted to do was storm out of there in a blind fury. For two, he hadn't worked a normal hourly job, let alone a normal nine-to-five job, like, ever. He wasn't used to needing to stay there until the work day was finished concept.

Parker took a step back. "Are you doing okay here?"

"Yeah, there's a sandwich shop around the corner. I got something to eat already. I'm just watching TV, and I've answered a few work emails."

His stomach lurched. A guilt-stricken realization washed over him. He totally hadn't even asked Nori how she was able to get away from work in normally a pretty labor-intensive position. His mouth was dry. "Is everything okay with the museum? They're okay with you leaving for a little while?" he asked.

Kristin Helling

She nodded, smiling. "Of course. I've earned my time off. Plus, I told them it was a family emergency. Family emergencies are pretty high up there on the scale of reasons to suddenly need to take a leave of absence. Your mom, Parker, is my family too, now."

That hit him like a ton of bricks. Crushing sadness and elation all in the same breath. He looked up at her. "I love you."

She smiled in return. "I love you too. Now go back to work and do what you do best."

He raised his eyebrow. "What I do best?"

"Research," she finished.

He let that sink in, without fully understanding the implication of the single word. He nodded with a new-found confidence. She was right, anyway. He was going to Greysen to ask for his help. He could still receive the man's assistance without Greysen specifically knowing the circumstances. If he was going to go behind Parker's back and not tell him information, then Parker was going to continue to pretend he didn't know what he had heard and use him for his resources.

He gave Nori one more kiss, his palm on her cheek, then tore himself away. He looked around the nasty hotel room once more as he went to the door. "I won't be long. One night

103

and we are out of here." He placed his hand on the knob, then lingered a moment. He looked back over his shoulder at Nori and bit his lip softly.

She laughed under her breath. "I'm fine! Just go..."

Before he allowed himself to feel any more of the guilt that dominated the pit of his stomach, he left the room.

As he walked back towards the Humavision building, a little less enraged and a little more determined now that he had a plan, he thought about what Nori had said. *Research.* What exactly did she mean? She certainly wasn't referring to the impulsive decisions he'd made such as quitting his job and going to Paris. Or other scenarios and decisions he'd made surrounding those same ideals. *No.* She was talking about something he was good at. Really good at. Something he researched to no end to make sure he had the facts correct.

Writing.

She meant he was good at researching his work required to write a novel.

Brilliant.

Parker had been responsible for writing *The Idea Man,* a best-selling novel that highlighted the trials of Grice, or Greysen. He'd written his story and really made a name for that character as being a humanitarian inventor. Greysen was the hero of that story.

But now, now everything had changed. Greysen had assumed leadership of the company he'd been screwed by. That he hated.

But Noriana had pressed an idea into his head that he'd never even considered before: the story he'd written. The story he'd half-lived and lived through Greysen for the other half. It'd been proven time and time again that words, *his words*, could have power.

He needed to write the sequel.

TEN

PARKER

Parker slipped inside his office and shut the door. He'd managed to get into the building, up the elevator, and down the hall without anyone noticing him, apart from the security he'd had to pass through at the entrance, of course. Earlier, he hadn't cared about Greysen seeing him upset outside his office door. He'd almost *wanted* him to see it, even though he'd told Greysen he hadn't heard anything. But now, Parker would be glad to know that Greysen hadn't heard him. It would be better that way. It'd be more inconspicuous and give him time to collect information without Greysen suspecting anything.

Yet even as Parker ran through his plan in his mind, doubts crept in. What was the point of sneaking around, anyway? Why not just confront him? They had a relationship like that, right? What was the real threat there?

Perhaps it was because it appeared that Greysen might have known Parker's mom this whole time, and never once mentioned it. Not in all the time they'd spent with each other. Or... perhaps Greysen *did* really have something to do with her going missing?

Parker needed to find out what the connection between them was.

And he couldn't ask his mom, of course, because she was missing. He didn't want to ask Greysen now, because he was hiding things.

So he needed to poke around himself.

First, since he wasn't in the trusting kind of mood, he scanned around his barren office. Since he'd just moved in *today*, he hadn't had a chance to make it his own, if he'd even wanted to. But there was still some furniture inside there. The desk, of course. The computer. A standing lamp in the corner. A small table where he could put a coffeepot if he wanted. Two chairs. One on his side of the desk and one on the other for visitors.

He looked at the desk. *Hmmm.* Parker placed the palm of his hand up underneath the underside of the desk. It was possible, especially since he wasn't in the trusting mood, that there could be a listening device inside the room. Even if not, he needed to make sure. It wouldn't take but a few moments to check.

This was some spy shit.

After checking the desk's underside, inside each drawer, and around the chair, he moved out to the other side of the desk. *Nothing.*

He walked over to the lamp. The last thing in the room. He scanned the stand and up into the glass vase that surrounded the lightbulb. Just as he reached up and got his hand inside to feel around for anything unusual, his office door opened. He yanked his hand back and banged it on the glass. "Ow!" he breathed as he shook his hand and looked over his shoulder.

"Oh my god, I'm so sorry." The woman stepped back out into the hall and slammed the door shut.

Carrie. Greysen's secretary. He stared at the closed door, heart pounding from being *caught* in the act.

A moment later, she knocked.

He threw his arms up. "Well for Pete's sake, come in. You were already in here."

She opened the door. "What are you—?"

"Me? Oh, yeah I was, uh..." He looked from her to the lamp. "I was making sure it was an energy efficient light bulb. Living in France, I've become more environmentally conscious. America's behind, you know." He scratched the back of his head and brushed his foot on the ground.

She stared, her brow furrowed.

He snapped out of it. What he did in his own space was *his* decision. He didn't need to explain himself. "The question is, what are *you* doing coming into my office without knocking first?" He crossed his arms.

"I thought—" Something caught in her throat.

"You thought I was still out on lunch?" He didn't know if that was the case or not, but he was proud of himself for being so quick on his feet.

"I'm sorry, I should have knocked." She also crossed her arms, and held her nose high.

"Is there something I can do for you?" He went behind his desk and sat down, motioning to the seat across from him. She was nice. She didn't do anything to deserve him being a jerk to her, except it was sort of suspicious that she'd just barge into his office thinking he wasn't there.

She held out the manila folder she had tucked under her arm. "It's briefing materials for the marketing campaign we're starting to work on. I thought you'd like to get caught up."

He reached forward and took it from her. "You... couldn't email it?"

She pursed her lips. Her eyes darted behind her black-framed glasses, indicating she was beginning to get irritated with the way Parker was treating her. The thing was, he was *trying* to see if she was nervous. And it seemed to be pretty easy to ruffle her feathers. Perhaps he could use her as a pawn to get to Greysen. It was worth a shot. He didn't know where her loyalties lay, but he was pretty certain they were with her employer. She was his assistant after all, which meant she'd had to have spent a lot of time by his side. And if she wasn't loyal to him, she wouldn't have continued working for him. At least she cared for Greysen. Hell, *he* cared for Greysen.

"I did come down here for a... another reason," she said quietly.

He raised his eyebrow.

"I wanted to know why you were spying on Greysen... earlier."

He laughed and hoped it didn't sound nervous. *What the hell.* He'd *just* started his mission. But, no. She was talking about him listening outside Greysen's office to begin with. "I don't know what you're talking about. You mean when we ran into each other before lunch? I went to his office to tell him my fiancé and I couldn't do dinner as planned."

"Couldn't you have just emailed that?" She smirked.

His cheeks warmed. "I wanted to tell him in person. I'd just arrived here. I haven't seen him in a while. I'm not just another employee he's hired, you know. We're..." What *were* they? Old friends? That just sounded weird. He let the sentence trail off.

"Listen," Carrie started. She moved up to his desk and put both hands down on it. "I know you heard what Greysen was talking about on the phone—"

It was as if the walls in the room were closing in. Tunnel vision straight to her face. The heat moved to his neck.

"—and I want to help you." Her voice was low and strategic. Almost too strategic.

He narrowed his eyes and grounded himself once more. It was tempting, it really was. But once again, he didn't know where her loyalties lay. She could be playing him. She could have been sent here by Greysen to pry him for what he'd heard. And the truth was, he had heard enough. "I..." He leaned toward her. Almost too close. "...don't know what you're talking about." He enunciated every word. "Thank you for the file. I'll get caught up." He leaned back in his chair and pulled up his computer screen. Perhaps if he looked busy, she'd just leave.

She turned to do just that, huffing as she went.

"Oh, and Carrie?"

She stopped in her tracks, keeping her back to him, but her hand on the doorknob.

"Tell Greysen, if he wants to ask me a question, he can ask me himself."

Carrie made no reply, only left the office and closed his door.

He exhaled as he looked into all four corners of the ceiling. *Wow, this is exhausting.* But he was fairly certain that his office was not bugged. At least he'd have one safe place.

Next, he needed to figure out how he was going to get into Greysen's office. And he needed to make it quick, because he had to leave for Kansas City in the morning. He only had tonight to figure out what Greysen knew about his mother, and what their connection to each other was.

Parker received an email alert that Greysen wanted to hold a meeting for distribution at 2pm. That would mean he wouldn't be in his office at that time, creating the perfect opportunity for Parker to go in there and snoop around.

He waited in his office until a little bit after two, once he knew that Greysen, and Carrie for that matter, would be at the meeting, which was luckily on a different floor. Still, he knew there were cameras everywhere in this building, considering the amount of security at the entrance as well. He was going to have to make this quick and effortless.

Parker slipped back out of his office and walked down the hall, turning right towards Greysen's office. Nobody was in the hallway, which was a good thing. Doors were open here and there, but when he got to Greysen's doors, a set of double doors, they were closed. He listened for a moment, and then tugged on the handle. As suspected, they were locked.

He reached into his pocket and retrieved two small, brown bobby pins. Noriana was constantly leaving them everywhere. Before he'd left the motel room after his lunch break, he'd snatched the few up from the round table in their room. His intuition that at some point these would come in handy, was right. And now was that time.

He maneuvered the bobby pins into the key hole, rattling them inside until he felt it catch, then he jerked upwards with the audible click of the door unlocking.

I'm in.

He shook his hands, stuffing the bobby pins back in his pocket with a smile. He'd used to pick locks all the time when he was a kid. He and his brothers used to do it for fun, especially around Christmas time when his parents would hide all their presents in the closet in his parent's bedroom. Thing was, they kept that closet locked. Though it was no match for curious little boys. That, among other games he and his brothers would play, were the reason he'd gotten good at picking locks. And it was a skill he'd never lost. Who knew as an adult he'd be picking a lock to break into his employer's office to possibly steal information about the kidnapping of his mom? It was ridiculous. But here he was.

His adrenaline kicked into high gear. He was out of his body, energy circulating through his limbs. His breath quickened. *Where do I even begin? The computer.* He rushed over and pulled a flash drive from his other pocket. He'd just happened to grab it from the motel room when he pocketed the bobby pins. The flash drive held some of the files for his novel on them. But there would still be space available for him to steal some of Greysen's files to sift through later. He shoved it into the USB drive and stared up at the screen. It was locked. *Frriiiiiiiick. Of course it's locked.*

If there was anything Parker wasn't, he wasn't a computer nerd. He didn't know how to hack anything, and there was just too much information to even guess at what might be worth channeling. This would be impossible.

Footsteps approached the door.

Parker ducked under the desk, panicking inside as the footsteps stopped, and then continued down the hall.

He released a sigh of relief. *That was close. Too close.* He needed to get out of here. He stood up and scanned the room, frantically looking for anything that might give him clues. He was attracted to the shelves filled with different books. "I wonder if he has any classics... or are they just boring books for inventors," he whispered as he looked closely at the spines. One navy-blue bound book caught his attention. It was skinnier than all the others, so it stood out to him. It had a year on it, 1994.

But what caught his eye the most was the silver-embossed writing. It said the name of the high school *he'd* went to. The high school his parents had gone to. And 1994 was the year his mom had graduated. Why would Greysen have her yearbook?

Greysen had very few personal things in this office. Parker knew that was because he'd had to leave most of his things, if not all of his things, behind when he'd fled the country thirteen years ago. He knew that because he'd written that story. Greysen wouldn't have kept a yearbook of all things, would he?

Parker stuck his index thumb on the top of the book's spine and pulled it out. Could he steal this without it being noticed? He looked down at his phone. It was almost 2:45, and he needed to get out of there, before anybody came back from the meeting.

He'd tucked the yearbook under his arm and started for the door when he heard a noise from down the hall, through the cracked door.

"Shit!" he whispered, putting the yearbook inside his shirt, creating a rectangular shape under the fabric. He flew to the door and peeked his head outside. A group of people were at the end of the hall, headed this way. He saw Greysen emerge from the group, entrapped by the conversation.

Thoughts swirled inside his head of what he was going to say as an excuse for being in Greysen's office. His previously *locked* office. Just when the nausea had kicked in from the potentially awkward social situation, Greysen

117

paused and turned around to address someone in the group. Parker slipped out and closed the door as softly as he could. He looked back up at the group to see Carrie staring directly back at him. Wide-eyed, he shook his head back and forth.

Greysen started to turn back around, but Carrie grabbed him by the shoulder and kept his back turned. "Oh! I think you forgot something back in the room!" she chirped.

Parker perked his eyebrows. She was... *helping him*. Keeping Greysen distracted. *Why* was she helping him? Currently, it didn't matter. He needed to get out of there. It didn't matter how it was happening. Parker couldn't go back to his office, because that would take him towards the group. He needed to exit down the stairs on the opposite end of the hall. So that's exactly what he did, clutching his chest the whole time.

Thoughts and questions raced through his mind regarding the book against his chest. Why would Greysen have his mom's yearbook in his possession?

He wanted so badly to leave and go back to Nori. But he still had a few hours before the end of the day, and he didn't want to raise any suspicion, especially from Greysen. So instead of leaving and walking into the main lobby, he walked across, all the way down the hall to the opposite staircase and started his way back up. He'd just make a giant circle as he went back to his office, avoiding everyone and anyone that he could.

He finally got back to his office and closed the door, locking it behind him this time. He didn't want another incident like the one before where Carrie just walked in. *Carrie.*

Why in the world had she helped him? Was she trying to show her loyalty to him? He wasn't buying it, still. He kept thinking she was playing double agent. There was no motive for her to help him. And he couldn't believe she worked for Greysen but wasn't loyal to him. That made absolutely no sense.

He took the yearbook out of his shirt and placed it on the desk. He opened the book. Just like any normal high school yearbook, there were names and messages written all over the front panels of the book. He read a few of the messages, nothing quite sticking out like a sore thumb.

HAGS, HAKAS: Have a great summer, have a kick ass summer.

119

The problem was, none of them were written out to his mom.

"Grey, you rock! Have a great summer!"

This was Greysen's yearbook. *So wait, Greysen and Mom went to the same high school? The same... year? They knew each other! Way back! All the way back in high school.*

Betrayal sunk in. Greysen had never mentioned it.

And his mom... he was sure he'd mentioned Greysen's name in passing, and she'd never said anything about knowing who he was either.

Perhaps they didn't know each other went to the same school? It could have been just one big coincidence.

However, there was a feeling in his gut that told him it wasn't a coincidence.

Parker flipped through the pages until he got to the section with all the individual class photos. He scanned through the names until he came upon Dottie Herring, and he followed the row over until he landed upon his mother's photo.

Yup. He was very familiar with this senior photo. He'd seen it before, in his mom's book back home, as well as when they'd gone through old family photos.

Next, he searched back on the names down to the P's. Pents, Pierce, Price. Greysen Price.

He dragged his finger over to the third image. Yup. Of course he was much, much younger, but it was Greysen through and through. He wore a look of hope, as though he was at the start of his life. That boyish grin showed no signs of jaded experience or fight, because he hadn't gone to battle yet.

Parker flipped to the back of the book, where more signatures and notes were scrawled about. One caught his eye: *"Hey Grey. Best lab partner a girl could ask for. Keep in touch, Dot."*

Dot. That was his mom, all right. And they hadn't just known each other. *They were close.*

He let it sink in. Heavy in his heart. *What am I supposed to do next?* As if the universe had read his mind, and his worries, his phone dinged in his pocket. He immediately thought of Nori, but when he pulled his phone out, Stephen's name showed up. "Hey," he picked up.

"I hired the PI, but I want you to go with me to meet her." He didn't even say hello.

"Okay, I'll be there tomorrow like we discussed. I can go then. But listen, Stephen, I'm finding out some stuff here. Did you know any of mom's high school friends?"

There was silence on the line a moment. "No, not really. We could ask Dad. They were high school sweethearts, right?"

"Yeah, yeah they were." Parker scrambled, opening the yearbook once more. He flipped to the pictures and down to the R's. *Rubec. Rubec. Rubec.* Nothing. His dad was not in this yearbook. Or at least not in the same grade. "But they didn't go to the same school?"

"I never asked. Why have we never talked about this with them?" Stephen asked.

Parker shook his head. "No idea," he sighed into the phone.

"Why are you asking about this, Parker?"

"It's a long story. I never... told you what happened to me. But the guy who commissioned me to write his book last year, he's now my employer in Chicago."

"You've *moved* to Chicago?"

"No. Well, yes, but not really. I'm hoping to work remotely, but the headquarters is here. Anyway, my boss—I heard him talking on the phone. I think he might know something about where Mom is. And I found a yearbook in his office. I stole it. It has a note from Mom in it." Parker closed the yearbook and placed his hand on top of it.

"Why don't you ask him about it?" Stephen asked, as though it was the easiest thing to consider in the world.

122

"Well, there must be a reason he hasn't told me he knew Mom, right? Why wouldn't he just up and tell me? I'm not sure what would happen if I confront him."

"Well you have to! If he has any information, Parker..."

Stephen was right. Perhaps he should confront Greysen. That in and of itself, depending on how Greysen handled it, could say a lot about what their relationship meant to him.

What was the worst that could happen? He could get fired from this job that he hadn't even really started, for snooping and not trusting Greysen. Sure, he didn't have any money. But he could go out and get a different job like a real person. Like what every other person had to do.

"Parker?"

"Oh! Sorry, man. Right. Okay, I'll go talk to him. It's not going to be easy." His ear felt hot from having the phone pressed against it.

"Look, I know that you've been through a lot. But just get what you can use, and get home, okay?"

"Yeah, that's the plan."

They hung up, and Parker lifted his head up to look at the back of his door. *Get what I can use and get home.*

ELEVEN

PARKER

As he walked down the hall, he went over and over in his head what he was going to say and how he would act. Calculated, and prepared for anything. So he thought. He got to the doors of the boss's office and looked back and forth down the hall. His nerves made it hard to breathe. He surpassed that as much as he could with the anger he felt deep inside so he could do what he'd come to do. He'd reached forward to knock when the door pulled back. He retracted, shuddering from the surprise.

"Parker! What are you doing? I was just going down to grab something from the copy room—"

"I need to talk to you."

Greysen took his hand off the knob and backed up. The way he perked his eyebrow told Parker that perhaps he was acting strange.

"O...kay. Copy room can wait." He backed up and waved his arm into the room. "Come on in."

Parker followed suit and went into the room, hands stuffed in his pants pockets. One hand grazed his phone, the other gripped a pen. "And Carrie isn't around?" His eyes darted around the office.

"No, she's busy with other things. Why? Do you need her?"

"No."

"Oh my god, do you have an issue with her?" He propped a hand on his hip.

Parker stifled a small laugh. "No." He shook his head. If anything, he owed her for helping him earlier. No, right now he just wanted privacy.

"Are you adjusting to your new role?"

"Greysen! Just... let me speak. Geesh."

"Okay, sorry." Greysen leaned against his desk. "You want to sit?"

"Nope, I'll stand. I'm comfortable with standing... here. Right here." He rocked back on his heels.

Greysen nodded, crossing his arms.

He hadn't seemed to have noticed the yearbook was gone. If he had, he'd have already been questioning Parker. He wouldn't be acting like he didn't know why Parker had come to talk to him.

Parker could totally rip him apart right now. But that wasn't the strategy he'd come here with. He needed to continue to give Greysen the benefit of the doubt, all the while holding him under complete and utter suspicion the whole time. He wanted to give him one more chance to be truthful about the fact he'd known his mom and they'd been close friends.

"I'm having some... personal trouble," he started. "And I'm coming to you for help. I don't know what to do. And I don't want you to think I'm taking advantage of you, but I know that you have... resources, so I thought I'd come to you before I took matters into my own hands." He swiped his hand over his face.

"Oh?" Greysen seemed quite intrigued now, if he hadn't been before.

"You see... it's my mom." He watched Greysen's expression very closely for any sign of emotion out of the ordinary. Now that he watched him with a level of suspicion, he was more able to identify a feature that he may not have noticed before.

Greysen cleared his throat. "Okay, what about your mom, Parker?"

"She's gone missing. And I think she's in danger."

There was a silence between them as Parker studied him.

Greysen showed a level of concern, but nothing on a deeper level. "What gives you the idea she's—" He cleared his throat again, his gaze darting around the desk. "—in danger, as you say?" He reached over and grabbed a bottle of water that sat on the desk. He unscrewed the lid and took a swig.

Parker looked away. "Well, for one, she left her phone and purse at the house. And she'd never leave home without them. It's been more than forty-eight hours since anyone has heard from her. My brother contacted the police, and they're drilling into my dad as a suspect, when he's already devastated. They're saying she could have possibly left on her own..."

"Would she do something like that?"

"Hell no!" It almost *burst* out. *–and you should know that!* If Greysen knew anything about her, he'd know that was something she'd never do. Parker took his eyes away from his gaze and paced around the room.

"Well if you feel like she's in danger and was taken against her will, I'd be happy to do what I can to try and help. I do have some contacts in the police department in Kansas City. You know,

Humavision has a remote campus there. In Kansas City."

"What?" He stopped pacing and looked at Greysen. "There's a Humavision campus in KC? Why have you never told me this?" *Among other things.*

"Well it didn't really concern you." Greysen looked away from him.

"I'm from Kansas City." He pointed to himself.

"I get that. But it only has a few departments. So it's not like you could work there... it's mostly IT."

Parker nodded. He wasn't here to argue, and he needed to stay on-task.

Greysen sighed. "I'm sorry, I didn't mean to make it sound like it was none of your business. And I'm sorry your family is stressing about this situation with your mom. You know I'm here to help. Can you tell me some information about her so I can pass it on to my acquaintances? If anything, I can get the police to move this case to the top of the pile because I'm sure they're busy and just brushing it off on some overwhelmed detective."

Parker watched Greysen move around his desk and sit, grabbing a notepad and pen. "Uh, yeah. Okay. Well, her name is Dottie Rubec." He zeroed in on the calculated blink of Greysen's eyes. The crease that became more prominent between his eyebrows. "Her maiden name is Herring. In case that's important."

Greysen swallowed, his Adam's apple bobbing on his neck. So as not to do anything out of place. Anything out of the ordinary. And it was just weird. He was for sure dodging any fact he knew her. At all. Blatantly. Right in front of him.

He clearly had something to hide. And if he was hiding this big of a thing, what else was he hiding from Parker? Perhaps Greysen even had something to do with his mom's disappearance? Why would he hide this part of his life, when Parker already knew everything else?

"She's forty-eight years old," he continued. "Dark brown hair, like mine, with some gray throughout, but when we find her, don't tell her I said that." He smiled under his concern. "We're just real worried. This is definitely out of the ordinary. She keeps a quiet, normal life." Just speaking about her lodged a lump in his throat. He didn't realize once he'd stopped to think about her, it would get to him. *Focus, Parker...*

"Do you know anybody who may want to see her harmed?"

He shook his head. He didn't even want to think about that. He wanted to shout, *Do you?* But instead he said, "No. Dottie—my mom—is the sweetest lady you could meet. She'd invite a homeless man over for Thanksgiving dinner if she passed him on the way home." He thought about that. Perhaps that could be his mom's downfall. She was too nice. "But she also had her wits about her. Her intuition was, *is,* her best feature. Her superpower." *Damn.* He really missed her. Even though he'd had all this distance away from her for years now, as an adult himself, the fact he couldn't just pick up the phone and call her was really eating away at him. He stuffed his hands in his pockets and yanked them back out again. "I mean, she raised three boys. She could smell shenanigans from a mile away." He smirked. But then he snapped back out of it. He wasn't here to genuinely tell this guy about his mother. *Greysen knows all this.*

Parker had now completely stated her name out loud and Greysen only showed what seemed like false concern. He ran his fingers through his hair, stopping at the back of his head, then dropped his arms to his sides.

"Look, I will call my contacts as soon as you leave this office. What if we go down to Kansas City together tomorrow morning? I can take you to the remote office, we can meet with my contact at the police."

He hesitated, though an answer was necessary. "Okay. I have to speak with Nori first, but our plan was to head down there anyway after I touched base here."

Greysen nodded. "I'll plan for that, then. I can come pick you guys up. Where are you staying?"

"At a motel around the corner from here."

"Geeze. I'd have invited you guys over to stay at my apartment if it wasn't so small."

"That's okay." *Yikes.* How would *that* have been? It was nice of Greysen to offer, but it was becoming more and more apparent that he was possibly a liar who couldn't be trusted.

A knock sounded at the door.

"Yes?" Greysen called out.

A young man peeked his head inside, "Mr. Price? There's an issue in the quality control department. I didn't know if you wanted to look at it or not... I can tell them you're busy."

"Yes. Clearly. I'm glad you're smart enough to notice I'm busy."

Parker shook his hand to signal that it was okay, but Greysen talked over him. "You couldn't send this in an email?"

"I'm sorry, sir. I'll do that next time. This can wait."

"No. I want to see it. Because evidently, I have to do everything by myself if I want it done right. I'll be down there in just a moment."

The young man nodded vigorously, clearly nervous and ashamed, and shut the door.

What the hell just happened? Greysen was such a dick! Does the behavior come with the job? Who was that person? That humbled, altruistic, homeless man he'd met on the streets of Paris seemed nowhere to be found. The man who'd given up everything for others. It was like Greysen had taken on his ex-boss, Edrick's persona. Parker hated it.

He logged it all in his mind to write down later. Parker committed to himself to continue Greysen's story. "I'm... going to go. Tomorrow morning, ya?" He didn't make eye contact with Greysen. He didn't want to. It was awkward enough.

"Yes! That works. And hey, listen." Greysen grabbed Parker's arm.

Parker jerked back exaggeratingly and looked at his arm first, then Greysen. For some of this, it was hard to play that he was okay with it.

Greyson must have been in his own world, because he didn't seem to notice Parker's knee-jerk reaction. He dropped his hand from Parker's arm but continued, despite Parker's look. "Listen.

I'm so sorry about your mom. Just from what I've heard, I, too, believe she did not leave of her own free will. We will find her, Parker. She will come home."

Parker nodded. His eyes welled up and the lump continued to remain lodged in his throat, but he didn't dare show that emotion in front of Greysen. He didn't deserve to experience the raw emotion. He'd lost that right of connection. After that brief moment, Parker left the office and headed back to his own to grab his stuff and get back to Noriana.

He inserted his keycard in the door and with a few beeps and the green light, he pushed into the small motel room.

Noriana was just coming out of the bathroom.

He dropped his bag and rushed over to her, hugging her and burying his face in the hair on her shoulder. He unloaded everything that had been building inside him throughout the day. He cried and cried, letting all of the pent-up emotion release onto his fiancé. He clutched her as she held him, and they collectively moved to the bed.

"I'm sorry you had such a hard day," she cooed softly into his ear.

He backed his shaking body from her and rubbed both his eyes. "I just miss her."

She nodded.

"We have to go to Kansas City tonight," he stated, regaining his bearings.

"Not in the morning?" she asked meekly.

"Greysen... he wants to drive down there together in the morning. He's expecting to come pick us up from here. I want to be long gone before he does. I want to beat him to Kansas City."

"You want to drive—not fly?"

"Yes, it's only about nine hours. If we start tonight, we can get there before the morning. We can go to my parent's house at three am. I can notify my dad or my brother." The air felt lighter now that he had some sort of a plan.

She nodded. "Why don't you take a shower, Parker."

"Do I stink?"

She laughed. "Even in these dark times you keep your humor."

He looked down at the bed. He couldn't help it. These things just blurted out of his mouth.

Noriana lifted his chin with her petite hand. "No. Whenever I have a bad day, it's nice to take a shower and wash all the day's worries down the drain. Come out clean, refreshed, and renewed. It's a psychological thing. But it really makes me feel better."

"That sounds good." He stood and pulled his shirt off over his head, tossing it on top of his suitcase on the floor. He unbuttoned his jeans.

"While you're in there, I'll contact rental car places and see about getting us a car for tonight. I'm sure this motel has a shuttle to a rental car place. If they don't, we can rideshare." She stood and searched around for her phone.

"Thank you, Nori." He walked to the bathroom as he removed more clothing. He screeched on the water and felt under the tap until it grew warm enough, then pulled the plunger to send the water up to the shower head. "Hey Nori?"

She looked up from her phone that she'd located on the table. "Hm?"

"When I get out, I can tell you what happened today. Why I want to leave instead of going with *him*."

"It's okay, we'll have the whole nine hours in the car to chat." She smiled softly at him.

She was right. She was always right.

They pulled into his parent's neighborhood. It was still pitch-black outside, with just the headlights from the car. In just a few hours, Greysen would stop by the motel to find that they'd already checked out and were long gone. Surely, it would piss him off. By then, he'd also be able to confirm any suspicion that Parker was onto him. Surely by then, the lies would haunt him. If he wasn't naive, that was. That fact just made Parker's pulse pound even harder.

He parked in the driveway, then turned off the lights. He hurried out of the car and over to Nori's side, opening the door to let her out. Then, he took out his phone and texted his little brother that he was there. Nobody these days knocked on the door. It was always a text. Especially at four in the morning.

Parker was exhausted, but none of that mirrored the look of his father when Parker walked through the door into the kitchen and saw him sitting at the table. He rose, and Parker gave him a hug, while Nori stood back.

"We'll find her, Dad. People don't just disappear." It was the only thing he could think of to say at the moment. Nothing else seemed right. No jokes seemed right.

His dad nodded.

"Mr. Rubec." Noriana stepped forward and offered her condolences.

"Please, please just call me Davis." His shoulders hunched forward.

Parker wanted to tell his family so badly that he and Nori were engaged. But it wasn't the right time.

Someone burst through the kitchen door.

They turned to see Stephen step through the doorframe into the kitchen. "Brother..." he breathed, pulling Parker into an embrace.

Parker coughed from his grip.

"Geezus Dad. You not sleeping?" Stephen wore green medical scrubs, and approached his dad, looking him closely in the eyes.

"How am I supposed to? We're going on almost seventy-two hours she's..."

Stephen placed his hand gently on Davis's shoulder, shooting a look back at Parker and Noriana. "I know. But you need to sleep so you can have sharp thoughts, okay? Parker's here now and we're going to work with everything we can. You aren't helping by not taking care of yourself."

Davis nodded.

"Here," Nori stepped in, "why don't I make you a cup of herbal tea and we can go sit on the couch? You don't have to sleep if you don't want to, but we can just chat and rest." She looked over at Parker for approval.

He smiled at her, his cheeks warm. She was a beautiful soul. She always knew exactly what to say. He loved that about her. She wasn't awkward, like he was. She was perfect.

Davis put his hand on Parker's shoulder as he exited the room. "It's good to have you home," he said quietly, and then continued into the family room with his head hanging.

"You guys have chamomile or something?" Nori asked quietly, walking toward the counter with the microwave.

"Top right cabinet, above the coffee pot," Stephen answered.

Parker blinked at his brother's easy answer. It'd been so long since Parker had been here, or visited with any regularity, he wasn't entirely sure where things were in the cabinets anymore. Some things changed, some things never did.

"You didn't have to come so early, Stephen," Parker said as they each took seats at the table.

Nori puttered around in the kitchen, heating water and gathering the mug and tea. When she was finished, she headed into the dim family room.

"I just got off a shift. I've been at the hospital all night. I was going to come here afterwards, anyway," Stephen finished.

"I texted Marshall, but he didn't respond. I forgot I had a key. He's most likely sleeping upstairs," Parker said.

"He's been withdrawing. He doesn't have that go-getter motivation like you and I."

"It's nothing new." The third brother was always the one who stayed at their mom and dad's the longest, and dropped out of school. Well, Parker had dropped out of school, too, but he'd still made something of himself. He'd still gone on to travel and do what he was passionate about. It seemed like Marshall didn't want to do anything but play video games all day in his room. But Parker knew Marshall was also worried about their mom and wanted her home, too.

"You should really try to get some sleep yourself," Stephen said. "None of us can be on our top game if we're exhausted. I know it's already the next day, but you should try to power nap. Around seven, we can go meet the PI I hired."

Parker tried to calculate in his head when Greysen was expected to pick them up at the motel back in Chicago. He needed to have a one-up on him at all times. Seven AM should work. He nodded.

"I'm glad you're here," Stephen whispered. "I can't keep this family together alone."

Parker hadn't realized it had come to that. He'd always viewed himself as the failure. His

140

doctor brother getting his PhD and making the family proud. But Parker was done with the mode of thinking that he just wasn't enough. He *was* enough.

And now, his brother, the golden child, was looking up to him. Grateful for him and his experience to help bring their mom home. He *did* have life experience and travel experience more than anyone else in his family to crack this case. He was a valuable asset. He didn't need to prove this to anyone, and he wasn't trying too hard; he almost didn't want to be in this role, to be honest, the role where he needed to step up and show up. Protect the ones he loved. Potentially, the role he was meant to do.

"You're not alone," he assured Stephen, and then dismissed himself to the family room.

Noriana stared off into the distance there, cupping her mug of tea with both hands. His father had dozed off on the couch. Parker actually smiled at that, grateful his father was able to get some form of rest.

"Let's go to the guest bedroom," he whispered to Nori. "Try to get some sleep before the day. We have about three hours."

She nodded, set her mug on the end table, and rose from the chair.

141

He put out his hand for her and she took it softly. He led her down the hall and up the stairs quietly to the bedrooms.

He shut the door with gentle ease behind them and put his bag down on the ground, sitting on the bed. He pressed the palms of his hands into his eyes. When he opened them again, Noriana stood in front of him in her underwear. He smiled, taking her by the hips and pulling her closer.

She crawled onto the bed with him and they laid back. She ran her hands through his hair.

"I'm glad you came with me here, Nori," he whispered, turning his head and kissing her on the collarbone. It gave him chills to touch her smooth, flawless skin with his lips. He stayed a moment, breathing into her chest.

She tilted his chin upwards and kissed him on the lips. It was deep, consuming in every way.

The rest of the world melted around him. *I should be sleeping right now.* But feeling her body and moving in sync with her was all the energy he needed right now. To feel the connection of another human as they made love. To feel Noriana. His fiancé.

He must have fallen asleep right after, because his phone alarm went off at 6:45am.

He'd gone into a deep sleep, even if only for a couple of hours, and now he rolled his stiff body off the bed, rubbing his eyes and then his hair.

Nori still lay on the bed, pulling the blankets up to her neck, over her naked body, and let out a big yawn. "It's time?" she asked.

"Yes, we're going to go meet the PI. You can stay here, though. Get some more sleep."

She sat up. "Parker. I thought we've gone over this already. I'm coming with you."

"I know, I know... but, maybe you should be here with my dad? I can call you with the news we get? It might be better if he's with someone, you know?"

She sighed. "I can do that. I don't mind. I just hate leaving you every time."

"I know..." He grabbed a shirt out of his bag and pulled it over his head. His hair was full of static from the shirt, and a small thought crossed his mind that he needed to get his hair cut. It was growing out, and he looked like a slob when he let it grow out.

"Parker..." Nori said, her voice more ominous than usual.

"Hm?" He looked back at her.

"I have something for you."

For some reason the tone of her voice made his heart speed up. Should he be worried? His intuition told him yes. What was she doing?

She slipped out of bed, wrapping the afghan around her body, and inched to her bag. She knelt down and pulled something out.

When she turned around, Parker jumped back. "Whoa."

She held out a little black revolver.

A chill crossed his shoulders and he straightened his spine. "Where did you get that?" he asked, remembering her father's gun and all that had happened at her parents' cabin last year. Nothing good could come from a gun.

"When you were at work in Chicago, I went out and got it. Did you expect me to stay in that stinky motel all day? Anyway, I went to a retailer. It's safe. It's not like I got it off the street or something."

Wide-eyed, he nodded and questioned how she could act as though this was something completely normal. Like she'd gone to the supermarket to pick-up milk and bread.

She walked over to him, opened and spun the cylinder to check the rounds, then snapped it shut again and held it out for him.

"How did you..." He'd never seen Nori handle a firearm like this before.

"My dad. He took me to the gun range growing up. He'd never keep a gun in the house without teaching his daughter how to safely handle one. This is a six shooter, double-action revolver."

Parker raised an eyebrow and nodded as he carefully took it from her. Perhaps education was the key here. *I guess it depends on* whose *hand it fell into.* But that did explain a lot and made him feel better about the whole thing.

"I don't know much..." He knew nothing. Her *dad* had trusted him also. But he'd just used that one for looks last time. Perhaps he could use this one for looks too. Just to scare his attacker. *Well, hopefully there won't be an attacker in the first place...*

"I can teach you. And we don't know what you're heading into, right? I just want you to be safe."

"Thank you for thinking of me," he mumbled.

"Put it... in the crease of your spine, in your pants. You can easily access it there." She helped him secure it in the jeans he pulled off the floor and put back on. He put his arms around her, hugged her, gave her another kiss, and then backed up.

"I have my phone. I'll call you when we're done talking to the PI, or if I have any other news."

She nodded. "We make a good team, Parker Rubec."

He smiled. "Indeed, Future Mrs. Rubec."

TWELVE

GREYSEN

Greysen sat back down at his desk, going over in his mind what had happened just now between him and Parker. And the annoyance of Michael coming in and telling him about issues in the quality control department. Of course that was the department that Molly had used to run, but he hadn't heard from her since she'd creeped in on him at his apartment. He was so caught up in the moment that he'd treated Michael like crap, and right in front of Parker, too. Michael didn't deserve that. And what did Parker think of him now?

He groaned and laid his head down on his desk. Surely Parker thought nothing of it. Surely, he was more concerned about Dottie missing. Parker's mom. What had happened? Of course Greysen had already known there was a possibility she could be in danger, since he'd seen the black-hooded figure contacting her in Edrick's memory. But how could they have even known he'd sent that locket to her? And he hadn't known they'd go as far as kidnapping her. *They.* Who were they, anyway? Clearly it wasn't someone who had a stake in Humavision legally like he'd originally thought, but they'd definitely had a hold on Edrick. And that meant there was a possibility that they could have a hold on him as well.

Only they hadn't shown up yet like he'd thought they would have by now.

He was tired of this and he needed answers. What was next? Did they, whoever *they* were, threaten Edrick's entire family? Everyone he loved?

That's impossible, Edrick didn't love anybody.

But surely, he must have. Someone, somewhere. *Corin.* Was it that at one time, he *had* had a family, and people he cared about, but the consequences of his actions made him chase them away? He'd become the hard soul that he was to protect them? He'd had to. And ultimately, it had ended in his demise.

Tomorrow, Greysen would head to Kansas City with Parker to start getting to the bottom of all of this once and for all. He'd been on journeys before with the kid, but this one... this one was different. And he didn't even know why. He hadn't thought this part of his past would ever surface, but here they were.

It wasn't just the IT department that was housed in Kansas City, but an important part of his past as well.

Greyson was smart. And when he'd seen the memory involving Dottie, and the mysterious shadowed figure on the screen making orders, he knew he needed to figure this out. He couldn't have whatever Edrick had been involved in threatening innocent people. Threatening people he cared about...

Maybe he couldn't figure out *who* it was, but he could potentially figure out *where* they were.

He lifted his head and woke up his computer.

Perhaps it wasn't as complicated as he was making it.

He'd hoped that all clues pointed to the person in the video speaking to Edrick at the time was located in the same place that Dottie had been. In Kansas City, Missouri. And if they weren't, they were going to have to reach out to him soon, because that's where he was going to be.

Greyson couldn't get Dottie out of his mind. He sat at his desk slumped over, neglecting all duties he had to get done for the rest of the day. He needed to make sure she was safe. But why? All those years ago, she'd ruined him. She'd crushed him. She'd set the mood for the rest of his life.

There were only a few things he'd saved from his home before he'd fled the country twelve years ago, and all of his belongings were completely repossessed. One of those things was in his office right now. On his bookshelf. He'd totally forgotten about it. And it was completely ordinary, unless you knew to look for it.

He stood up and walked over to his bookcase, scanning the shelves.

It wasn't there.

He ran over the spines with his eyes again, more frantically this time.

How?

It would mean nothing to someone coming in here and looking for things to steal. It was too... hidden. Too particular, yet unremarkable.

Unless... it'd been taken by somebody snooping, who it *would* mean something to.

Parker.

No one else could have possibly cared anything about an old yearbook. But how would

Parker have gotten access to this office? He couldn't have swiped it when he was in here talking just an hour or so ago. Parker *had* been acting strange then. Antsy. But then again, his mother was in danger and he'd seemed nervous to ask Greyson for help. But he had also accepted the help, in the end.

Had Parker known the implications of the yearbook he'd taken?

And why wouldn't he mention something about it? Unless... he was testing me. In that case... I failed the test. I didn't tell him I knew his mother all those years ago.

Greysen tensed, his mouth going dry. His muscles felt rigid and tight.

Because if Parker truly did have that yearbook in his possession, then there'd be no doubt he'd know Greysen and Dottie had had a relationship back in high school.

That would be the extent of it, though. There was no way he'd know anything more. And he'd agreed to the road trip to Kansas City tomorrow. That would give them a lot of time to talk things out. Greysen needed to take tonight to think about what he would say.

He turned to his desk and picked up the phone. He dialed an inside extension. "Can you come to my office at your earliest convenience?"

"I'm a little busy, Mr. Price. We talked about this. We can make a meeting for later."

He huffed. "No, just, what are you doing tomorrow, Carrie?"

"I'm working. Just like I do every day." Her voice was strict and studious.

"Okay. Tomorrow, you're coming on a business trip with me and another colleague. We're going to Kansas City."

"Would that colleague be... Parker Rubec?" she asked slowly.

"Yea! Is that a problem?" A lump caught in his throat.

"No, sir. I'll pack my bags tonight and meet you here in the morning."

He nodded reflexively, though she obviously couldn't see him through the phone. "Bright and early."

"Okay, sure. I need to get back to work now. It's a mess down here in this department."

"So I've heard. Can you handle that? I'm not in the right mindset right now. I might take the rest of the day off to prepare for the trip. Oh, and Carrie? Do you know if anyone may have had access to my office at any point in time in the last twenty-four hours?" He furrowed his brow, leaning on the desk with his free hand.

She hesitated. "No." Her voice was sing-songy, a few octaves higher than normal.

"I locked my office when we were at the meeting earlier, yes?" *Parker wasn't at that meeting.* Sometimes in his daily life, he did things in his subconscious mind. Like driving home, then realizing he couldn't remember the route he'd taken. Terrifying, but security in this building was never something he'd had on autopilot. Surely he would have remembered to lock his office.

However, this kind of security was different. This wasn't something sensitive within the company. This was all personal business.

"Are you missing something, Boss?" she asked.

"Uhh..." This time it was his turn to hesitate. "I'm sure it's fine and I've just misplaced it. Thanks. See you in the morning." He hung up the phone before she had a chance to respond. Mostly because he wanted to avoid the questions that might follow if he told her what object was missing, and why he thought Parker was the one to take it.

Before he got a chance to start anything new, his door opened. Greysen looked up to protest. *What is Michael doing back already, I told him I'd go to quality control myself!* But when he looked up with his furrowed brow, it was not Michael standing at his door.

"Oh, hello? Can I... help you?" he asked the man standing in the doorway.

The man stood there looking like a pirate. Dark beard, pocked skin, and a bomber jacket. He reached his hand up to his mouth and yanked a toothpick from between his teeth, tossing it aside as the light caught the chunky gold rings on his fingers.

The tightening in Greysen's gut told him this wasn't going to be a pleasant conversation.

"You're gonna be the one beggin' for help here in a moment." The man's voice was gruff through his thick black beard.

Confirmed. How did this guy get in here? Greysen couldn't help but stare at the ink above the guy's left eyebrow that read "haunted", with a small teardrop tattoo underneath his other eye. Everyone knew what that tat meant: this man had killed someone in prison. A real winner here.

Greysen swallowed hard. "What do you want?" He'd just been thinking about this possible encounter. Now that it was here, he just wanted to run. He didn't want to find out what sort of mess Edrick had been in. He didn't want this baggage, if that's what this was about.

The man lifted his arm to show a black duffle bag in his grip. He approached Greysen's desk and dropped it with a hard thump. "You are to bring this with you when you go to Kansas City in the morning."

They've been listening! Greysen's eyes darted around the room a moment before they fell on the bag. *What's in there?*

The man turned on his heels and made for the door.

"Wait! Why? I at least have the right to know what I'm doing this for. I'm not Edrick! You can't just move on to the next person because he's dead." Greysen had to catch his breath. He tried to hide his chest from rising and falling too much. *I'm too old for this shit.*

The man stopped, then turned to him with a smirk. "Don't shoot the messenger. I just do what she asks. And there's a reason she keeps me on the payroll." He pulled back his jacket to reveal a gun strapped to the inside. "I'm... persuasive."

Greysen nodded, wide-eyed, to signify the message had been received. Then, he didn't take another breath until the man had left his office, closing the door behind him.

He sat in his chair, dumbfounded, weak in every muscle. *How the hell did he get into the building? Is there someone in security that is in on all this?* There was no other explanation for it. He reached forward and pulled the duffle bag to the edge of his desk. His fingers slightly trembling, he slowly unzipped it.

Packed to the brim, were stacks and stacks of cash.

Cold, hard cash.

Clearly this was some sort of drug operation. Money laundering, perhaps? He made a mental note to go to the accounting department when he got back from Kansas City to poke into their profit and loss history. He'd never paid attention to it before. He'd trusted those hired to take care of it. That had clearly been a mistake.

The accountants could also be involved in the cover-up.

Though many things had stuck out to him in this recent exchange, one flashed across his mind over and over and over again since the moment the man had said it: *I just do what she asks.*

She.

The *persuasive* tattoo man who'd barged into his office was just the messenger. And his boss... was a woman.

THIRTEEN

GREYSEN

It was morning already, though still dark out, and Greysen pulled the car up in front of Humavision. Carrie stood there with her weekender bag by her feet, and a large black suitcase next to her. She wore a camel-colored trench coat and nylons. She always looked so professional, even when they were about to embark on a nine-hour road trip. Perhaps because she wanted to compensate for how young she was. She always dressed as though she were older, though she was definitely half Greysen's age.

She didn't need to do that for him. Greysen respected her for the hard work she put in, not for her age or any other irrelevant factor. Though of course, he could never bring that up, because then it would be at the forefront of her mind.

"Morning, Boss," she said, moving to the back of the car.

Greysen popped the trunk from the driver seat and pushed open the door to get out. Though when he reached the back of the car, Carrie had already tossed her own bag in, next to the black duffle, and made her way back to the passenger side.

"You want to grab the suitcase? It's heavy with the memory machine in there." She slammed the door shut.

He nodded, rocking on his feet for an awkward moment before he followed suit. Greysen wheeled the suitcase to the back and carefully lifted it into the trunk. Then, he rounded the car and sat in the driver's seat. He sighed and then took a side glance at her.

"What, did you want me to sit in the back or something?" She motioned to the back seat.

"Oh, no, sorry." Greysen snapped out of his trance. "No, Parker has a guest. His fiancé. She's coming along for the ride. I figured the two of them could ride in the back."

"His fiancé?" she asked, emphasizing the word. She placed her travel coffee mug in the center console cup holder.

Why didn't I think of coffee? This looked like something she'd brought from home. Surely, if she'd gone out, she would have texted him to ask if he'd wanted anything. More importantly, did the sound of her voice imply she was interested in Parker? It indicated she was definitely surprised he was promised to someone. And the fact that they were here, even.

Greysen hadn't sensed any chemistry between the two of them. *Guess I'll find out soon enough, being stuck in the car together for so long.* But then, Carrie most likely would never act on any feelings, if she had them, when Parker had his fiancé right here with them.

Greysen hit the gas, easing onto the road. The motel was just around the corner.

"I've already canceled all your appointments, so you shouldn't be needed here. Of course, look at your email periodically for the blueprint prototypes to come back for approval. But it's not time-sensitive." She pushed her glasses up on the bridge of her nose and poked at her phone in her lap.

He was grateful she was on top of everything. All this personal stuff was weighing him down. Of course, was it really personal when he strongly suspected it was somehow directly linked with Humavision?

He pulled in front of room seventeen. The hunter-green door was directly in front of the car and he killed the headlights. A housekeeping cart perched adjacent to the car. There were no other cars around, although Parker had said they'd taken a rideshare here, hence the reason Greysen was going to drive.

Just as he was about to get out, the maid pushed the cart to the next door, Parker's door, room seventeen. He watched through the windshield as she placed her keycard in the door and propped the room open. Greysen and Carrie could see just inside, the bed with the sheets slightly askew, and an otherwise empty room.

"Are you sure he said room seventeen?" Carrie asked quietly, as though she was almost afraid to voice it.

"Yes!" He was sure Parker said room seventeen. An uncontrollable heat rose in his throat. He squeezed his eyes shut a moment and opened them again, then took a deep breath in. "Hang on." He got out of the car and slowly approached the door to the room, standing back a bit so he didn't scare the maid. "Excuse me?" he asked softly.

The woman lifted her head up, alarmed, though acting as though this may be a common

160

occurrence. "Fresh towels? Shampoo? You can just take them off the cart, sir. It's fine."

"No, uhh, no thank you. I was just wondering if the people staying in this room are gone? Have they checked out already?" He already knew the answer.

She hesitated.

Was it against motel policy or something? Still didn't hurt to ask.

"Nobody is in this room now. I'm doing my daily morning rounds."

"Thank you. Have a nice day." He doubled back to the car, so he didn't spook her anymore. He definitely didn't want to make anyone uncomfortable. He slammed the car door shut behind him. Without looking at Carrie, he put the car in reverse. 'They freakin' stood us up. I should have known." He straightened out the car and continued onto the road, trying his best to avoid an audible peel-out.

This was going to be a long car trip. He pulled out his phone and handed it over to Carrie. "Can you call him?"

She opened his phone and held it up to her ear. After a moment: "Voicemail."

"Keep calling him," he urged through a clenched jaw.

Moments went by.

"How many times do you want me to do this?"

He muttered expletives under his breath. "He knows." *The yearbook.* He sped onto the highway on-ramp, entering into traffic. They needed to get out of the city before rush hour.

"Knows what?"

"It's a long story."

"We've got nothing but time."

He snuck a glance over to her. Perhaps it would be to his benefit to clue Carrie in on what had been going on, and why in particular they were taking this business trip. She may be of some help to him, after all.

Hours went by as he explained everything. Pouring the story and his entire life out to her was so rejuvenating, so therapeutic.

When he was finished, he inhaled deeply, keeping his gaze on the road ahead.

Carried sighed.

"What? Have I spoken too much? I'm sorry."

"No, that's not it. It's just... I have to confess something to you."

His throat constricted. *Uh oh.* That was never good. Especially after he'd just confided everything, well, mostly everything, to her. Did she have something to do with the money laundering through Humavision? He waited for the worst. "Did you know they were leaving before this morning?" he asked.

"No, I didn't know that. But, uhm." Her voice shook. "I did… help Parker do something behind your back, though."

"Oh?" He wasn't sure he wanted to know.

"He was in your office yesterday," she spat out quickly. Everything about her body language, the way she slouched in the seat and turned her head away from him toward the window, said she regretted what she'd done.

"When? How?" He wasn't mad. More inquisitive, if anything. And actually relieved it had nothing to do with the duffle in the trunk.

"When we were coming back from the afternoon meeting, I saw him leaving your office. You would have seen him coming out, but I distracted the group."

"By saying I forgot something…" He furrowed his brow.

"Yes. I don't know why he was in there… or how he even got in. Because I know you locked that door before we went downstairs. But the look on his face when we were coming back—it just told me he needed me in that moment."

"Why? Why would you go against our trust to help someone you just met?"

"I don't know! Like I said, the look he gave me.... It just felt right doing it in that moment. I knew you guys were close. I thought maybe he wanted to surprise you with something, or something like that. I didn't think he'd do anything to hurt you."

He almost let the question slip as to whether or not she had the hots for Parker, but he bit his tongue. That was rude. And inappropriate for a boss to ask. And irrelevant. "Well, I think I know why he was in my office. The yearbook. It was gone. He must have seen it, discovered the information about Dottie inside it. That we were together."

"I know."

His gaze shot over to look at her. "Wait? How do you know that?" He stared a long moment before he forced his eyes back to the road. His muscles tensed.

"Greysen..." she breathed, "I didn't know he took the book, but I knew what was inside it... when we were reevaluating the prototype of the Memory Machine these past few months—you know I had to go under myself as well, right?"

"You... watched my chips?" *There's no other way she'd know something as personal as my relationship with Dottie.*

164

She breathed a rattled breath. "Are you mad?"

He didn't know what to say. They were locked in this small box on wheels for several more hours. There was no escape. And even if there was, what information did Carrie now know about him that she could use against him? To her advantage?

He lifted his hands off the steering wheel and then slammed them back down. Now he was thinking crazy. Carrie wouldn't think like that. Would she? He'd just offered up most of his life story to her moments ago. How much of that had she already known? He didn't even know anymore. "How many researchers watched...?"

"Nobody else watched them. Just me. They're safe, Greysen. And I didn't watch very much. Just enough to get the experience going under. I didn't have anybody else to go off of. Watching my own memories doesn't have the same effect. You know that. There wasn't much for me to pull from once we deemed the memories extracted from the employees under Edrick as unethical." She took her glasses off and rubbed her eyes, then put them back on. "And plus, it... it helped me get to know you better. On a different level. I think I've been able to provide more effective assistance to you than somebody who doesn't know anything *real* about you. Wouldn't you say? I promise it's strictly professional. Nothing more."

He nodded, but his throat was dry, and his abdomen cramped. He needed to piss. He didn't know what to say and they coasted down the road in silence.

"I'm sorry," she squeaked underneath the hum of the highway.

"It's... it's fine, Carrie. You're right. I just feel vulnerable, is all. I think it has led you to help me better than any other assistant I could have ever had. I wasn't sure if it was that you had a natural way of handling situations and personalities, specifically my personality, or what. I do appreciate the work you do. Just... it's awkward, is all. And I'm quite upset that Parker has an idea of who I am, but he doesn't know the whole story. I imagine he's scared and confused. I just want to solve all this."

"So... is that why you had me pack up the entire memory machine in that suitcase and bring it with us?"

He squirmed in the seat, then stretched his neck back and forth. "I think it could work. If I can convince Parker to talk to me, maybe he'll agree to go under and watch the memory of his mom and I. Maybe that can help him understand."

Carrie nodded.

They continued along the road in silence.

But after a while, he had to ask. He had to be sure. "And you're telling me you didn't know anything about the duffle bag full of money or the man with the tattoos I told you about?" He was almost afraid to ask. But she was the only one he could continue to hold any sort of trust in, despite everything.

"Honestly, no." She sounded surprised herself. "You said he mentioned his leader, the one he answers to, is a woman? Greysen... do you think it could be—"

"Molly? It's been on my mind since he left my office." He pursed his lips after that.

There wasn't much else they could do before actually arriving in Kansas City. And even though he held that duffle bag in the trunk of the car, his main focus was on his personal vendetta.

Greysen had an inkling of the first place Parker would go, he just hoped they got there in time to catch him. Especially if Parker hadn't been answering his phone.

Another indication that the kid was not happy with him.

FOURTEEN

PARKER

I t'd taken a moment to find a parking spot. This small metro just ten minutes north of Kansas City was bursting with charm. Historic buildings ran along its Main Street, shadowed by a huge, Hogwarts-looking university. It took on the persona of a Colorado mountain town, minus the mountains entirely. The coffeehouse sat in the middle of it. Built in the 1800s, it was the watering hole of the town.

But there were never any parking spots. They finally found one in the public lot across from some train tracks at the far end of Main Street.

"We're on time," Stephen proclaimed, putting the car in park and turning off the engine. "Parker, I hope we get some answers meeting this PI. It doesn't feel real. I feel like we're spies or something trying to find help from other sources

169

other than the police. Is this your world now?" he asked.

Parker gave a small chuckle, despite their situation. He'd had that same thought before. "More or less," he joked, though it wasn't really a joke. It *had* sort of, kind of, been his world the last couple of years, but all by accident, certainly. He got out of the car and started walking towards the buildings.

Stephen caught up.

"You look weird when you're not wearing scrubs," Parker stated.

Stephen laughed. "Yeah, that's my life, all right."

Stephen had a great job. He loved helping people. But he also had a wife at home. No kids yet, but they planned on having some before too long.

Does Noriana want kids? My god, they'd never talked about that. That was something they probably should have talked about before he'd asked her to marry him. Parker wanted kids. Perhaps they could start with a dog first, though.

He'd decided, after mulling it over on the drive from Chicago and now again on the drive here, he'd just go ahead and work for Humavision until another opportunity came up. He didn't want to continue working for Greysen.

170

At this point, it was just way too complicated. They hadn't even mapped out what his schedule would be, anyway. If he would be able to work remotely or if he'd have to spend all his time in Chicago—which was what it seemed he'd have to do. That was something they should have hashed out in the very beginning. He felt Greysen was stringing him along.

Stephen looked down at his watch. "So the PI said they'd meet us here at the top of the hour. We're right on time."

As they walked up the brick sidewalk, past a pizza shop, Parker asked, "So how did you find him?"

"Uh, *her*, actually. Not him."

"Oh, okay! Cool." That was actually pretty awesome. *A female PI.*

"And one of the surgeons at the hospital gave me the referral. Said she works freelance and was really down to earth. But has a reputation for never failing a case."

Parker opened the door for his brother, going in after him. The coffeehouse was cozy and narrow. They squeezed through a group of runners to get to the counter.

"What do you want?" Stephen asked, his wallet out. He ordered for himself.

Parker overlooked the bags of coffee on a shelf next to the registers. "Just a couple of shots of espresso for me."

Stephen told the barista, paid, then moved down to the end of the bar to pick up their drinks. He looked over his shoulder. "So fancy. Look at you, all European and such," his brother teased.

Parker shrugged. "I guess you could call it an acquired taste."

Stephen smirked. Their drinks came up and they made their way to the stairs. Rickety and dodgy looking, the stairs were numbered up to nineteen. Of course, with how ornate this shop was, it wasn't surprising to Parker that the number thirteen, an unlucky number, was missing. Was it intentional? Either way, it lent to the charm of the place and he wasn't sure why he didn't spend more time in here when he'd lived here. After all, he'd pretty much spent all his time in coffeehouses, trying to write something good.

"She said she'd be up here?" Parker whispered underneath the soft hipster music. There must have been a speaker just above them.

Stephen nodded, first to Parker, and then toward the back of the upstairs. A woman sat in the far corner by a window that had an overgrown aloe plant on its sill. The entire upstairs of the shop was furnished as though it were a family room in the 70s, with orange couches and a bead divider hanging from the ceiling off to the side.

The woman didn't look the way Parker had imagined her. How would a PI look, anyway? Black trench coat? Sunglasses? This woman wore jeans and a plain, gray t-shirt. She had a red scarf wrapped decoratively in front of her shirt.

"Hi, uhh, Priya Blackwell?" Stephen asked, and they approached her apprehensively.

She smiled and stood to shake his hand. "Yes, you must be Stephen Rubec then?" She pushed her auburn bob away from her shoulder.

"Indeed. And this is my brother, Parker."

Parker stretched out his hand and shook hers. Firm grip.

"Pleasure." She nodded to him. "This is a nice little spot." She sat back down in her seat, across from Parker and Stephen.

"Thanks for meeting us," Stephen said.

She nodded. "I'm sorry it's under these circumstances. I understand that your mom is missing?" she asked. Her tone was genuine.

Parker saw it in the way her eyebrow quirked. She had great bedside manner, considering her line of work. Some people just had that kind of energy inside them. Honestly, it was a gift. "Yes," he said, "we've been working with police. But they're not taking us seriously." He looked over his shoulder at the others in the upstairs. Just one other couple was up there, in a small sitting area by the beads. The music drowned out the couple's conversation enough that Parker felt it was enough cover for them as well. Stephen had said she was a freelance PI, so she must not have had an office they could go to if she opted for a public location.

Priya nodded again, sporting a facial expression that suggested, 'go figure'. "Let me guess. They gave you some schpeel about how grown women go missing all the time? And how ninety-five percent of the time they left on their own? It's a load of bull, in my opinion. It's them telling you they have a lot of work to get done, and that your mom's case will sit in a stack of paperwork on their desk. Ugh. I'm sorry, sometimes I go off on one of these tangents. I apologize."

"No," Parker interjected. "You're exactly right. That's exactly what's happened to us."

"Listen, I'm here to help, okay?"

Parker still wasn't sure whether or not she could really help them, but he was willing to try anything. Especially if he ended up being wrong about Humavision having anything to do with it.

But then... what he'd eavesdropped on when Greysen had been on the phone the other day was just too much of a coincidence for it not to matter.

Stephen shifted in his seat, lightly butting Parker with his shoulder to most likely wake him out of his trance. "Well, you came highly recommended, so I'm glad you're available."

"Thank you," she said. "I have done a lot of missing persons cases. But you're going to have to work with me to let me know everything there is to know that could potentially help me." Priya pulled her phone out of her pocket and placed it on the coffee table between them. "Do you guys mind if I record? It's a little more conducive to taking notes."

They nodded in unison.

"Okay, uhh—" Stephen started before Parker got the chance.

Though Parker wasn't entirely sure what he could even reveal to her that wouldn't sound like a conspiracy, so he was happy to let his brother talk for now.

"Well, my dad said he went to go pick-up a prescription at the convenience store on the corner, and when he came back, she was gone. He had the car, so she couldn't go anywhere by car unless somebody picked her up, as they only

175

have one vehicle. And she didn't bring her phone or her purse, with her wallet in it. None of the neighbors saw anything. And our younger brother was home at the time—upstairs, but he says he didn't hear or see anything."

It took everything he had for Parker not to roll his eyes. Of course. But on the other hand, his other brother was probably beating himself up about that, as well. "Of course Marshall didn't hear anything," Parker breathed. "He's so clueless all the time."

Priya checked the recording on her phone. "No, it's good. It's good he didn't hear anything because that tells us that there was no big struggle. At least not inside the house. And if she went outside on the front porch or driveway, or even back behind the house, you'd think a neighbor or someone else would have heard something. Now, do you guys know if any of your parents' neighbors have a doorbell camera or other security cameras?"

"We could... ask my dad?" Stephen asked.

"Okay, yeah. I will need to talk to him as well. I know you're the one who hired me, but the more of the picture we're able to get, the better." Priya reached forward and picked up her phone.

"I can get you guys in touch," Stephen said.

Parker's throat was tight. His head swayed. "Hey, I'm going to go to the bathroom. I'll be right back. Anyone need a refill?" He asked, smothered and suffocated by the conversation. His head was anywhere but here. They shook their heads and he grabbed his empty mug and made way for the stairs.

It was nice and thoughtful of Stephen to hire a private investigator, but there wasn't anything she could do that Parker couldn't, in his opinion. And he already had a one-up on her. From the moment he found out from Greysen that there was a branch of Humavision located in Kansas City, he'd an inkling of where he could go to look for his mom. And he was wasting his time here, when he should have been following this lead, and figuring out the connection between her and Greysen. And whether he'd been chosen by Greysen to write that book on accident... or on purpose.

When he got to the bathroom, he closed and locked the door, then leaned back against it. The gun in his pants pinched his lower back. He pulled out his phone and called Nori.

"How's it going?" she asked.

"I mean, the detective is nice and all, but I'm wasting my time, Nori." He spoke in a hushed tone, nervous about the echo in the bathroom.

"I need to get to the Humavision campus and poke around. Even if it has nothing to do with Mom, I need to rule it out. Why would Greysen hide the fact that he knew my mom, and also the fact there's a campus in KC? And If anything, he should be here soon. He's been calling me non-stop."

"Have you answered?"

"Psh, hell no."

She chuckled. "Well, your dad's in good spirits."

He closed his eyes. "Thanks for keeping him company."

Someone banged on the door. Parker flinched and backed away from it. "Someone's in here!" he called out. They banged again. "Jeezus!"

"Are you... in the bathroom? That's so unsanitary, Parker!" Noriana joked.

"Alright, I better go. I'm going to try to go to the Humavision building once I leave here, okay?"

"Just... be careful."

"I will, bye." He hung up and flushed the toilet to make it seem like he'd had a reason to be in there.

He opened the door to see an old lady standing there. *An old lady? Come on.* Judging

178

by the banging on the door, he'd have thought it was a kid or something! The nerve some people had.

As he walked towards the stairs, he saw Priya and Stephen standing outside the large front windows. He changed course and headed that way, leaving out the front door and thanking the baristas working as a bell chimed.

"Hey, Stephen," he said as he stepped out onto the sidewalk, "I'm going to call a rideshare. I have somewhere I need to go before I go back to the house. It's, uhh, for my new job." He wasn't lying, but he also sort of was. He couldn't let them know the suspicion he had. He wanted to find out for himself. For multiple reasons. One, he wanted to be the one responsible for finding his mom first, so he could ask her the burning questions that had been haunting him since he'd found that yearbook. And two, he didn't know for sure yet that Humavision was even involved. It was just a guess. If he led the PI down the wrong path, he'd be wasting her time and taking her away from what actually could have happened to his mom.

"Oh, go ahead and take my car, man. I'm going to ride with Priya down to the police station to get an update on their status, so she knows where to start."

"Oh, okay! That works out then."

Stephen handed over his keys. "I'll see you soon, okay? I'm glad you're back in KC."

"Hey Priya, it was nice to meet you!" Parker said, then he turned and walked towards the city lot, past the train tracks to get to his brother's car. When he sat down in the driver's seat, he felt the gun again as it hit up against his lower back in the seat.

Well, at least he'd have something if he ran into trouble when he went to the building by himself. It was a matter of protection.

He pulled out his phone and googled the address to the Humavision KC Campus building. It was actually on the Kansas side, in Leawood. That made sense. It seemed as though they were always developing that area, building it up.

Parker double-checked his pocket for his new Humavision employee badge. He felt the outline of the card and exhaled quietly.

As he drove along the highway, with the voice of his GPS calling out commands in an Australian accent, he thought about the conversation he'd overheard from Greysen's office.

"Why would I see that in Edrick's memories then, huh? When I fled, they had to cover all their

bases? But I was for sure they'd never find out about her."

Greysen must have seen Parker's mom in Edrick's memories. What was the memory? What could he have seen?

Parker struggled and pushed back against the mind constriction and tightness in his throat. His chest burned with frustration. After all this time and everything they'd been through together, why couldn't he just trust Greysen enough to ask him directly?

Because Greysen lied to me. He broke all trust. He's obviously hiding things from me. Parker balled up his fists. Well, if Greysen was going to hide things, then Parker wasn't going to be able to ask him anything. Because what would stop Greysen from lying again, or telling Parker anything but the truth?

He swerved onto the exit ramp.

As he pulled into the parking lot, he cased the joint. Nothing looked out of the ordinary for a weekday afternoon. It was an office building. A neutrally boring facade on the outside. He pulled out his Humavision lanyard and badge. Surely he could get past anyone without raising suspicion. It was the fact everything else about this was unknown that made him hesitate. What was he getting into? And why was he feeling the need to do this on his own?

He had the help of the cops, and his family, and now this PI, Priya. But no. He *needed* to do this on his own. He felt like it was personal at this point. It was, indeed, personal.

The hesitation quickly smothered beneath the weight of his why. The reason he was diving head-first into the unknown was to find his mom. And every minute longer she was missing was another minute closer to the possibility of never finding her.

He leaned forward over the steering wheel a heaved a sigh. *Never finding her...I can't think that way.* If he suppressed, it was easier. Being numb...was easier. He squeezed his eyes shut, then opened then again.

He got out of the car and walked toward the building, scratching the back of his head and looking around for surveillance cameras. He wondered if the security was just as tight at this facility as the one in Chicago.

The cold, hard metal of the gun in the back of his pants stalked his thoughts. He wouldn't be able to go through any security with a weapon. Well... he'd cross that bridge when he came to it...

He pulled open the glass door and found himself in a reception area, and a woman with gold cat-eye glasses sat behind a counter. There were no metal detectors, to his immense relief, and behind the half-moon reception desk was a huge facility of cubicles, separated by faux corkboard walls.

"Can I help you, sir?" She was cordial, professional, and wearing a suit.

He was dressed down, for sure. Why hadn't he thought about that? He'd been so flustered this morning, and when he was flustered, he tended to make mistakes. *Play it cool...* "Hi, yeah. It's my first day." He held up the lanyard with his photo ID on it.

She looked confused, and then typed vigorously into the computer in front of her. "Name?"

"Parker Rubec." Should he have chosen an alias in the heat of the moment? Most likely not, since his name was attached to his file anyway.

She sighed. "Chicago must not have gotten the information over to me."

"Oh, you're not prepared for me?" He was operating by the seat of his pants, here. He raised his voice but kept his cool.

"No, no we are surely ready, Mr. Rubec. I'll guide you to the orientation room and have your mentor meet you there."

He smiled, and the tension in his jaw relaxed. "Thank you." He wiped his free hand, the one without the lanyard, on the side of his pants.

She came out from behind the desk, staring into her computer once more and then awkwardly glancing at the lanyard he dangled by his side. She held her neck stiff and opened a half door to the left of the desk. "Right this way." She had a sudden nervousness about her that he hadn't noticed at first.

Parker couldn't tell if it was from his moment of treating her as if she were incompetent when it wasn't her fault, or whether it was because she was just socially awkward altogether, which was unlikely. But it was the IT department, after all, although she was also the face of the department, the secretary, for lack of a better word. Surely they would have hired someone with great people skills for that role.

He followed her through the door, and kept a close eye on everything they passed, all of his surroundings. It was like a maze between cubicle walls and desks despite the open floor plan. Everyone quietly clicked at their keyboards or talked into their headsets, not paying any attention to him or the receptionist.

He looked at the receptionist's hand that dangled by her side as he followed her. She was tapping the tips of her thumb and middle finger together repeatedly. The notion set nerves in the pit of his stomach, and he looked around for different doors and rooms his mother could possibly be held in. It didn't seem likely. If it was, it was a hell of a cover. But Parker had heard of Humavision's production value from Greysen, and he wouldn't put it past them.

"Ah, we're here," she said, opening a door that led to a bare room. A single table sat in the middle of the room with a few chairs around it. The walls and table were bare.

The moment he walked into the room, he wanted back out. There was something about the energy here. The florescent office lights made him want to turn and run. They were too harsh, too bright.

Maybe they reminded him of his former life, before he'd dropped everything and gone to Paris for the first time. That time of his life was something he definitely wanted to keep in his wake. It reminded him of the times he'd felt worthless, a loser. Now, he'd traveled and through that, he'd found himself. He knew who he was, what he wanted, who he wanted to spend the rest of his life with, and what kind of life he actually wanted. And he wasn't sure if that was him just growing up, or if it was all the stuff in-between then and now that had given him his strength and purpose.

Whatever had happened to cause it, Parker was grateful for the change.

He walked further into the room and turned back to the woman, who still stood out in the corridor. "What room did you say this was?"

"Someone will be with you for orientation shortly," she said abruptly, and then shut the door.

Well that was weird... He went to the door and tried to open it to call out to the woman and repeat his question. But the door didn't budge. Parker tensed, fear shooting through his gut. That couldn't be right. The door shouldn't be locked... He tried the knob again. "What the hell..." He yanked on it. *Locked. It's locked!* "Hey! Why did you lock it?" He banged his fists on the door. Panic engulfed him. His palms grew sweaty, and his heart raced. "Hey!" His voice echoed back in the small, windowless room, and somehow, he knew that nobody on the other side could hear him.

She had been onto him. She must have been. Why else would she lock him in here? Perhaps Greysen had already been here first.

I knew I wasted too much time talking to that PI! Should never have agreed to go with Stephen in the first place... not going to need her anyway, clearly...

And now he was a sitting duck in this room. Greysen could appear at any moment.

He pulled out his phone. First instinct. He had no bars, and no service. "Shit!" It was like this room blocked all cellular data. He wouldn't be able to call out or go on the internet. He put his phone back in his pocket. He examined the door knob. There was no key hole on this side of the door, so he wouldn't be able to pick this one like he had with Greysen's office door. There was the other thing in his pants... the gun. He could take it out and shoot the door frame, blasting out the lock. But that would make a ruckus. And that was the last thing he needed when trying to fly under the radar to find his mom.

Mom!

The reason he was here.

If they could lock him in a seemingly soundproof room without phone access, they could do the same to her.

Parker was not about to sit in this room just waiting.

The more and more he hesitated, the more the walls seemed to close in on him and the air grew thicker and thicker. He looked for vents in the room. Was the air being sucked out? He breathed heavily, trying to calm himself, but the anxiety had already manifested in his being.

His gaze floated upward. The ceiling had rectangular tiles, like those he remembered from grade school. He stepped up onto a chair and then the table, gaining height enough to be able to push up on one of the ceiling tiles. It was exactly how he remembered. And there happened to be a big support beam that ran straight through the middle of the room, inside the ceiling. If he could get up there... that could be his ticket out.

He jumped back off the table, took one of the chairs, and dragged it over to the door. He wedged it up underneath the doorknob. He needed more time.

They didn't want him getting out, and he didn't want them coming in, either.

Then he grabbed another chair and put it on top of the table, relieved in the moment that these chairs didn't have wheels like most conference room chairs did. That should be

188

enough leverage. He crawled onto the table again and then on top of the other chair, slowly standing. It put him about a quarter of the way into the ceiling, and that was enough to pull himself up, onto the support beam.

He was grateful for it, so he didn't fall through the ceiling tiles as he tried to navigate. He looked all around the dark and dusty inside of the ceiling, seeing bits and parts of the infrastructure of the building. If he followed the ventilation duct, he could make his way out. He could also potentially use this advantage to search other rooms in the building.

Greysen might have been the master at escape and going on the run, but he'd underestimated Parker. Parker had gotten rather good at it, himself, since... well, for pretty much his whole life.

When he'd been probably nearly two, he was playing Legos with his cousins in their bedroom. Their parents were in the family room talking and not paying attention to the little kids, most likely relying on the older kids to keep an eye on the younger ones. But they were kids, too. So they hadn't done a very good job of it.

Parker remembered then what had happened next. He held onto the support beam in the ceiling as the scene flooded back to him.

Two-year-old Parker got bored. He crawled off through the bedroom door and into the hallway. He looked down the hall to the light in the family room. It was boring down there, too, but it was then that he spotted it. A slide. There was a stool pushed over the top of it, but because he was already so close to the ground, he just lay his head down and turned his neck to rest his cheek on the ground. Ta da! There it was, nestled underneath the stool. The top of the slide.

He used his meager strength to push the stool just enough for him to squeeze into the hole in the floor.

"Weee!" he cooed in delight as he went down the dark slide. It was really dark. And when he got to the end, there was no way out. And no opening to escape like usual.

"Ma!" he yelled out, and his voice echoed through the metal tube. "Mama!"

He obviously couldn't remember how long he'd been in there, as he couldn't remember much of the ordeal since he'd been so young. Most of his memory of it was more the recollections of other people than his own memories, his mom and cousins, telling him what had happened that day.

He called and called for her to come, and eventually heard lots of commotion.

"Parker! Baby! Oh my god, he's in there, Sherry."

He heard their voices on the other side of the slide. He giggled and looked above his head at the light.

He'd been told they'd had to call the fire department to come and cut him out of the vent pipe. He imagined being inside that vent pipe was sort of similar to hanging onto this support beam inside the ceiling of an office building as he replaced the ceiling tile back into its fitted spot like the last puzzle piece. It was pretty dark and dusty up here. He lifted his shirt up over his mouth and nose and coughed as quietly as he could into his chest.

He listened for a moment, just to hear if they'd come back for him in the room yet. Though with locking the door with a chair, he'd given himself just a little more time.

Parker inched forward on the beam, until he became comfortable with moving along it, if that was even possible. When he'd assumed he'd moved over about two rooms based on the size of the room he'd left, he reached back and pulled his phone out of his pocket. The light from the screen lit up the whole inside of the ceiling.

191

He wouldn't be able to use it frequently, for fear that the light might shine down through a vent or something and catch attention.

But a quick glance was enough to see that he still didn't have any service, so he stuffed it back into his pocket and moved on. He inched further, until he heard voices directly underneath him. He froze. Still as could be, he perked up his ears.

"What do you mean?" a male voice demanded. "How the hell could he even get out?"

"I don't know, sir," another voice answered, this time a woman. "We put him in a contained room, like you said. We locked it from the outside, so he couldn't get out..."

Parker squinted into a crack on the edge of the ceiling tile. He could make out two people below.

"He can pick locks."

"This doorknob doesn't even have a peep hole for the lock or anything, though." The woman's voice was panic-stricken. Parker was unfamiliar with it, but he was pretty sure it was the front desk lady's voice.

The other voice was obvious. Not only because he'd known it now for years, but because of the loads of voicemails left on his phone in the last twenty-four hours, and because of the context clues from the woman speaking to him. That voice had authority, and she was scared. Greysen was here.

"Well did you search him and take his personal affects?" Greysen asked.

"Well no, sir. If we'd done that, it'd raise suspicion, wouldn't it?"

That bastard... Parker wanted to burst through the ceiling and land on his shoulders, yanking Greysen's head from side to side. He visualized it so clearly. But he didn't. Instead, he laid in wait.

He honestly didn't know where to go from here, anyway.

"Well get searching! He couldn't have gone far. I mean, there's no windows in that room, and he didn't go out the door..."

Parker saw them through the tiny crack in the ceiling tile as both their gazes raised up toward him.

"You don't think—" the woman started.

Shit! Parker started to inch away on the beam. And then it happened. First, the vibration in his pocket. He shuddered. And then, the song started.

It had been the theme song for Wiley Coyote and Bugs Bunny.

He fumbled to get it out of his pocket and hit the side of the phone to silence it, nearly losing his balance and falling off the beam.

It was as though it had all been planned. He'd totally forgotten he'd set that ringtone as a joke. It was no joke now.

"I knew it!" Greysen yelled. "Get a chair," he barked at the receptionist. Then he looked back toward the ceiling. "Parker! I'm not... I'm not mad, okay? We just... we need to talk! Please!"

Oh nooow he's going to try and be nice? Just talk? Ha! No way. Parker army-crawled as fast as he could through to the next room, then decided to change direction. The beam didn't go that way, but there were thinner cross beams he could crawl on, along with piles of spiderwebs. Hopefully none were poisonous. Most likely their homes hadn't been disturbed, well, ever.

Spiders? Come on. They were the least of his worries. He was being hunted by something much scarier at this point.

Humans were scarier than any other monster out there, any day.

Parker removed the ceiling tile and looked down, hovering over a round toilet bowl inside an individual stall. Luckily, nobody else was in there. That would have been awkward to explain. He used his arm muscles, now violently trembling from needing their strength the whole time he crawled through the ceiling, to move his lower half down through the opening. Shaking, he placed his feet on the slippery porcelain of the toilet seat. Once balanced, he let go of the ceiling, not bothering to close it back up as he sat down on the toilet a moment and just took a breather. He exhaled, patting his body all over as if he needed to make sure he was all in one piece. He was still quite tense, but in a much better position than he had been up in that ceiling. Though he knew they were looking for him, he took his phone out of his pocket to see who had been the one to blow his cover.

Noriana.

He hit redial.

"Where are you?" she asked before he could speak.

"In the toilet." He couldn't help it. The opportunity for the joke was gold. "I'm in the Humavision office, but Nori, I need help. It's a long story, but they locked me in a room and I escaped but—"

"No, I know you're in the Humavision building. But where? I saw Greysen and a girl get out of a car and go inside."

"Yeah, he's here. Are... you?" It was a stupid question. He got the gist.

"I've got a car and I'm on the left side of the building from the front door, right now."

"Oh my god, Nori! I'm in the bathroom, there's—" he pushed open the bathroom stall door and peeked around. There was a window on the brick wall. "There's a window. I think I can crawl out of it. Just drive around until you see me, I guess?"

"I'll be there. Hurry."

He hung up and pocketed his phone. His adrenaline continued to run rampant.

Parker unlocked the window and yanked on it, pulling it sideways. The hole was small, but he'd fit. He heard a click, what he thought was the bathroom's door handle being turned, and froze. But nobody came in, so he used what strength he had left to pull himself through the window headfirst, just as Noriana's car rounded the corner of the building. She zoomed up as he pulled his legs through and sprung them in front of himself, hopping to the ground. His hand bolted to the back of his pants. The gun was still secure. He yanked open the passenger door and eased in, then Nori pressed the gas.

Parker leaned back in the car seat and closed his eyes, heaving a huge sigh of relief.

He'd done it.

He'd made it out. "You're the hottest getaway car driver I've ever seen," he said to her, smirking.

"Why are you so sweaty?" She laughed.

He reached the back of his hand to his forehead and swiped it. "Because that's the most working out I've done in ages." Another wave of relief washed over him as he looked in the rearview mirror. The Humavision office building became smaller and smaller, and when they turned onto the double highway, he was officially safe. "How did you know I was still here?" he asked.

He remembered a time when he'd questioned whether Noriana was with or against him. He'd even thought *she* was his stalker in Paris when he'd first met her. How far they'd come since then!

She shrugged. "After Stephen came back to the house and I still hadn't heard anything from you since you'd called me from the coffee shop, I got worried. I used Find my Friends, and it tracked you there. Were you looking for Greysen?"

"No, actually. I thought there might be a chance my mom was there. But it's really just an office building. The IT department is housed there or something. Something where there are a lot of cubicles. There weren't that many rooms around the perimeter. I mean, when I heard they had a remote location here... I got hopeful. I keep thinking, what if Greysen has nothing to do with my mom's disappearance, after all?" He leaned his head back on the seat and sighed, then shook his head. "But... then there was that phone call I overheard... and now I know that Greysen and my mom knew each other in high school, and they were close. And I think... I think maybe some bad people are after Greysen, and they took my mom as leverage against him. They must have found something out that pinpointed them to her. I don't know what though."

Noriana focused on her driving and was smooth and precise with it. "Then why not work together with Greysen to try and get her back?"

Parker cracked open the window and closed his eyes as the breeze hit his face. "Because I can't trust him. He's known me for several years now and he said nothing about knowing my mother. Not once! Don't you think that's a little suspicious? And then, when I gave him the chance to come clean, to admit he'd known her... he still said nothing! I have a feeling there's more to it than I know, but he doesn't seem to want to talk about it. What else will he lie to me about?"

She nodded. "Well, Parker. I have some good news for you."

He lifted his head and looked over to her, his stomach flipping as though he'd rounded the hill on a rollercoaster.

"That wasn't the *only* Humavision building in Kansas City."

He kept quiet and listened.

"There's another. A little google stalking and down an internet wormhole, I found a warehouse they used to use for production of prototypes. It's been shut down for years now. It's in some area called the West Bottoms."

If it weren't for the shock of both hope and fear that shot through Parker at this news, he would have laughed at her question. Of course. Everyone from Kansas City knew where the West Bottoms was; an area known to have several old, abandoned buildings. The ones that hadn't been rehabbed into a haunted house or antique shop.

A perfect place to hide someone.

"We have to go," he whispered.

Nori turned to grin at him. "I'm already headed that way."

FIFTEEN

PARKER

Noriana shifted the gear into park, right there on the potholed street, not even pulling to the side or into a parking spot. "Okay, it says it's this one right here." None of the buildings were marked, of course.

Parker had never been to this part of the West Bottoms. This part had alleyways that you'd be stupid to go down if you valued anything about your life. He'd experienced a few of the haunted houses back in high school with some friends, but that part of the West Bottoms was frequented by people quite often, and it wasn't so bad when lots of people were around. "All right," he squeaked, then cleared his throat and took a deep breath to steady his nerves. When he spoke again, his voice sounded more normal. "Let's go in, then."

Noriana grabbed his arm and he sat back. "I think you should go in without me, and then use me for backup," she said. "If we both go in, we're abandoning our car and risking us both getting caught."

He nodded, his nerves gearing up again. But he tried to put on a brave face for Nori. "Okay. Yeah, I like that. Safer for you, anyway."

She rolled her eyes. "That's not what I was going for. And it won't be safer anyway if I have to come save your ass again."

He laughed. "Well I didn't want you involved to begin with," he huffed.

"Oh come on, you know I love to come save your ass."

He leaned over and kissed her. "I love you, Nori. I'm glad you're here."

She batted her eyelashes. "I know. Now take that gun you don't know how to use and go see if your mom is in there."

"What makes you think I don't know how to use it?" He raised an eyebrow.

They both snorted.

He pushed out of the car and looked around, then headed for the building. The obvious choice of entry would be the front, and he wanted to avoid that at all costs, just because that seemed the most logical way. Before he disappeared into the darkness of the alley between that building and the next, he glanced over his shoulder to see Noriana pulling out with the car, most likely going to hide out of sight.

He continued into the shadowed alley and patted the weight in the back of his jeans. He looked up at the dilapidated brick building, seeing the caged fire escape scaling the side. There was a dock in the back of the building, with a ramp and a garage door. If he stepped up on that dock, he'd be able to possibly jump to the fire escape. From there, he could gain access into the building from one of the higher floors.

Parker walked over to the dilapidated dock and climbed up on it. It was a pretty far jump, but it was worth a try. He bent his knees and then leaped toward the bars, grabbing onto them and swinging in mid-air, just like his days doing monkey bars on the playground. His armpits felt like they'd rip out of his body, and he couldn't swing here long, so he grunted as he pulled himself up with his arms just enough to grab the next rung on the ladder. First one palm, then the other. At that point, the rusty ladder felt the pull, and began to descend down from its second layer.

Generally this would have been done from above, when trying to get out, or a fire truck would use their ladder to reach this one, if need be. Though he wondered now how they'd even get down the alley with a fire truck, anyway. It was much too narrow for that. Had they thought about those things back in the day?

The ladder descended down to the pavement, and Parker was able to touch ground, and then easily climb up the ladder all the way to the landing on the second floor. Once up there, he pulled the rusty ladder back up, just to cover his tracks. Just in case.

He peered into the fogged-up window of the second floor. It pretty much looked dusty and abandoned inside, with no signs of civilization. He tried to lift the window, but it was either locked on the inside or painted shut. He took the gun out of his pocket and looked around again one more time. He used the weighted butt of the weapon and smashed it into the glass pane, shattering it inside.

Pain seared across his forearm and he jerked it back with a yell, then glanced down at it. A piece of the sharp glass had cut him as he'd broken through it. Bright red blood seeped up to the entrance of the wound and he held his arm up to his chest, trying to use his shirt to dampen it. He swiped it and looked down. It wasn't deep, thank god. That's the last thing he needed right now.

He used the gun again to clear the glass around the frame, and then ducked his head as he stepped into the building. He stood a moment and listened. If someone was in here, they'd have heard him smash the glass, no doubt.

There was nothing. Not even the hum of a vent. Any move he made in this old abandoned warehouse would be heightened by its disturbance to the dusty old walls that just wanted to sleep in peace.

The floor he'd come in on was one large room, and he spotted a freight elevator with a set of stairs next to it. He rushed to the stairs, but did so as quietly as he could. Then the choice came, down or up?

Down had less coverage, he thought. He could check that out real quick before scaling up.

And perhaps he'd find nothing at all. Perhaps this whole trip to the West Bottoms would be a bust. The thought had crossed his mind that perhaps whoever took his mom wouldn't likely bring her to a Humavision building, even an abandoned one, unless they wanted her to be found by Greysen, which was a possibility. But Parker wouldn't know that unless he knew the secret Greysen was keeping from him about his mom. Regardless, he had to check out this building just to rule it out. Just to be sure.

Keeping the gun out and by his side, he went to the stairs and started down them as slowly as he could, so as not to make a noise. He used the railing where he needed, his legs shaking so badly at the knee from all the muscle work he'd had to do today.

When he came down the stairs, there were two levels to the first floor: a catwalk stretched around the perimeter that looked down on the floor below. In the middle of the raised walkway was a grand staircase that went down to the main level of the first floor. From his current position, he could see all of the ground floor. A pile of stuff in the corner caught his attention. He looked closer.

A mattress. Tattered blankets. Water bottles. *Someone* was staying here. There was no indication of who or where they currently were. It could have been a homeless person squatting in the building. Or...

Something shiny reflected by the mattress.

He hurried over to the stairs and pattered down them as quickly as he could, nearing the mattress. Connected to a beam that shot to the ceiling, and half-covered by some of the blankets, were handcuffs.

Someone wasn't staying here, someone was *held* here.

His throat constricted, and his knees grew weak as he thought of his mom.

"Freeze."

Parker shuddered. He was afraid to turn around, but he recognized the voice. "Can I at least stand up and turn around?" he asked Greysen. *Damnit, I should have been paying more attention.*

"Fine."

Parker stood from kneeling and slowly wheeled on his feet to face the man, but kept his eyes on the floor.

"Throw the gun on the floor and kick it over."

Parker narrowed his eyes. He didn't know what to do or say. He didn't even want to look at Greysen. He shuddered, his muscles locking up. *How the hell did I not hear him come in the building?* How long had Greysen been following them? It must have been shortly after they'd left the IT building, because he and Nori hadn't been here long.

Parker thought of his phone in his back pocket. He needed to somehow let Nori know he needed help. Or... perhaps he should do this on his own. He hadn't wanted to involve her to begin with. And why was he always wanting for help? He was fully capable. But...

Was Greysen armed? Parker had assumed so from Greysen's specific orders, but then, he hadn't actually looked to make sure yet. Part of him was afraid to look, afraid to see Greysen leveling a gun at him. Greysen wouldn't hurt him. Would he?

He'd done so many unpredictable things lately that Parker didn't know *what* he was capable of anymore. He swallowed hard and made himself look up, made himself lock eyes with Greysen.

His insides quailed at the sight of the weapon. Greysen *did* have a gun. And it *was* leveled at him. Parker's heart rate doubled again, nearly choking him. He tried to take a slow, deep breath, tried not to show the fear, but his mind raced, going wild. Who was this man standing in front of him, really? He looked so different from any of the other times Parker had seen him before, all cleaned up now and still dressed in a suit. His previously kind and open face now hard and stern, the blue eyes cold.

And holding a *gun*. Aimed straight at Parker.

Was this the *real* Greysen Price? Had Parker ever really known this man at all?

Parker licked his lips and made himself ask the question. "What will you do if I don't?" At least he sounded calm, somehow, despite his hammering heart. Despite the trembling in his hands, or the suffocating sense of betrayal closing in on him.

Greysen's eyes narrowed. "Don't make this hard, Parker. You're not going to use that. So drop it. I am not the enemy!"

"Oh yeah?" Parker dropped his gaze to Greysen's weapon and raised an eyebrow. "Then what the hell is that?"

"I have to protect myself, too. I didn't know what I'd find here, either. Or... or what you might do." He jerked his chin toward the revolver still gripped loosely in Parker's right hand.

Parker wanted to scoff, but he didn't think now was a good time to make it obvious he didn't really know how to use the gun.

"Parker," Greysen snapped. "*Drop it.*"

This time the tone of his voice sent chills through Parker's blood. He was *not* playing around. And he looked like he knew a lot more about firearms than Parker did.

Parker tossed his own gun behind him, towards the far wall, out of the way. Out of both his and Greysen's reach.

Greysen's lips thinned into a hard line.

Parker shrugged. "You said drop it. You didn't say where."

"I did, actually. I said *kick it over*."

"Oh. Must have missed that part." Parker let the anger seep into his voice. It was building now, that anger, warming his insides and melting away some of the fear. He'd trusted Greysen. Written his story. And suffered a lot because of it. And now for the man to turn on him like this...

"Smart ass," Greysen breathed. "Look, I told you, I'm not the enemy." He lowered his gun, to Parker's relief, and tucked it away in the back of his pants, hidden away behind his suit jacket. Then he held his hands out palms forward, seeming to relax. "I just want to talk things out, okay?"

Parker didn't buy it. He took a step back as Greysen stepped forward, but at his retreat, Greysen stopped again.

Parker had a bitter taste in his mouth. "Yeah? Then why have you been lying to me? And why did your employee lock me in that room, hm?"

Greysen shook his head. He dropped his hands and his shoulders sagged. He sighed heavily. "I told them to detain you, yes. You kept running from me, Parker. And all I wanted was a chance to talk to you... what else was I supposed to do? I've had to go to great lengths just to get you to give me a chance to explain myself, here."

Parker shook his head and backed up a few more steps, but then paused as he realized what Greysen had just said. *He needed to go to great lengths just so he could explain?* What was the extent of that? Parker was suspicious of everything now, straight back to the very beginning. "You mean like in Paris? The notes?" He blurted it out before he could stop himself.

Greysen opened his mouth to answer, but the warehouse's front door crashed open. Noriana stumbled into the dim central room, beams of sunlight darting into the room with her.

Parker's eyes went immediately to her forehead, where a line of crimson blood appeared through a part in her bangs and trailed down the side of her beautiful face. Quickly behind her emerged another person.

Carrie from Chicago. And she held Nori's right bicep tightly in one hand.

That didn't look like a friendly grip.

She must have come to Kansas City with Greysen. She'd managed to help Parker when

211

he'd been snooping around in Greysen's office, sure, but even at the time, he couldn't help but wonder what was in it for her. There must have been some ulterior motive.

If she'd really been on his side, why was she grabbing onto Nori like that?

"I *knew* you weren't on my side," he yelled at Carrie. "Let her go!" He switched his gaze to Nori, softening his glare into a look of concern. "Are you hurt?"

"You know her?" Nori asked, looking to Carrie and then back to Parker.

"She works with him." Parker pointed at Greysen without taking his eyes off the girls.

What if Greysen had cameras in his office? He could have seen Parker stealing the yearbook.

Parker's mind ran wild now in the heat of the moment. Before the girls had barged in here, he'd been about to find out if he and Greysen's meeting in Paris had been entirely premeditated. If Greysen had stalked Parker for more of a reason than just wanting him to write his story.

Greysen put up his hands as if in surrender. "Your side? There are no sides here, Parker. And what is he talking about, Carrie?"

Parker noticed then that Carrie also looked a little rough. The side of her pants were caked with dust, dirt, and pavement. The side of her arm was scraped up and her chin was skinned. "I told you in the car on the way, remember? When I said you'd left something—"

"What happened to your head, Nori?" Parker blurted, ignoring the conversation between Greysen and Carrie. "Are you okay?"

"I'm okay," she mouthed.

He read her pale lips, and his eyes trailed over to her arm, where Carrie's grip still looked tight. "Hey, let her go! What the hell is this? Noriana has done nothing wrong."

"*Nothing wrong?*" Carrie repeated, incredulous. "She hit me with her car!"

Parker's eyes widened.

Noriana pointed up to the wound on her head. "Steering wheel." She shrugged.

Boy, do I want to hear that story! But right now, there were other things at hand that needed to be solved first. Parker straightened, hands balling into fists at his sides as he tried to look as intimidating as he possibly could. "I *said*: let. Her. Go."

Carrie side-glanced at Greysen, who gave just the slightest nod, and she pulled her hand to her chest, releasing Nori.

213

Nori pulled her arm away and limped toward Parker, who took her into his arms and then turned her to the side. "You really okay? You dizzy?" he whispered, looking into her green eyes.

"Parker. There's something you need to see." Greysen's voice was faltering, unstable.

"Do you... have her?" Parker asked, shakily, breaking his gaze from Noriana and looking over to Greysen.

"Believe me when I say, *I don't.* I was sort of hoping she was here as well."

He didn't even have to say who they were talking about. They both knew, unspoken.

"Well she *was* here." Parker nodded over to the corner where the grimy, stained mattress and handcuffs lay.

Greysen spoke again, in a soft tone. "That's a pretty big assumption, Parker. We have no evidence she was here. That—" He motioned to the mattress and handcuffs with his brow furrowed. "—could be from anyone. We need to stop this back and forth between the two of us. I haven't been entirely truthful with you since we... met."

The angry energy inside Parker surged. Was he *this* close to figuring out what had been going on this whole time? He reached over, the back

214

of his hand knocking against Noriana's, and he moved his palm to close around hers. "You mean about how you and my mom had a relationship?" he asked, his throat dry.

Greysen stared blankly. "You know?"

That confirmed it, at least. Parker still didn't understand the extent of it, though. "I saw your yearbook. And her message to you. Just before I left for KC."

Greysen advanced forward.

Parker put his arm out. "Stop." He still wasn't ready to trust him.

Greysen stopped in his tracks. "I can imagine how spooked that must have made you."

Parker stared, wide-eyed. Spooked? Sure it had spooked him... it had spooked him Greysen had kept such a thing from him for so long, especially in light of recent events, with his mom going missing and all. He tightened his grip on Noriana's hand.

"I want you to go under," Greysen stated. He stared unfaltering at Parker. Determined.

"Why the hell would I do that?"

"Go under?" Noriana whispered.

Parker turned his cheek toward her. "The memory machine," he whispered back.

"Because I think you'll want to see what happened all those years ago between Dot—

215

between your mother and me. And I think it'll help us to find her."

It was that last line that hooked Parker's attention. He'd do anything to find her. *Anything.* And if that meant giving in to Greysen and working together with him, even if just for a little while, he could sort out his feelings about Greysen himself later. He took a deep breath and swallowed. "I've never gone under to see someone else's memories before. How safe...?"

The crow's feet by Greysen's eye twitched. He'd been quite familiar with the device. Maybe too familiar. Dangerously familiar.

"Parker, Greysen and I have both worked with the machine countless times," Carrie said softly.

Greysen nodded. "Carrie controls the computer whenever I have to use it. She knows what to watch out for as far as physiological signs of distress. She's aided me in going under more times than I can count. And when I've done it, it's in a safe and controlled environment. I think... you watching this will be the only way for you to understand."

Parker looked over to Noriana to gage the emotion in her face. She bit her lip with a furrowed brow.

Carrie spoke again with the same soft voice. "Nori can come, too. She can be by your side the whole time."

Parker looked back to Carrie, then to Greysen, and shrugged. "Fine. If it'll get us closer to finding her, then I'll do it. Show me what to do."

Greysen's body drooped as though a huge weight had been lifted off his aging body, just by Parker agreeing to experience his specific memory. He put his gun back inside a pocket of his jacket. "We need to go back to the IT building," Greysen said. "There, we can get a private, clean room, and all of our equipment is there."

"Why?" Parker demanded. "Why do you have the memory machine here in KC?"

"We brought it with us," Greysen admitted. "I knew it would come to this. I knew once Carrie told me you'd been in my office..."

I knew it. Parker wished more than anything he could get a drink of water to lubricate his throat.

"...I realized the yearbook was gone and that you perhaps had found out about our connection," Greysen finished.

Parker looked at Noriana again, who seemed to be in agreeance with him. If she wasn't, surely

217

she would have spoken up by now. He sighed. "Okay, let's go then."

"I'm going to have some of my guys watch over this building in case Dottie is brought back here," Greysen said. "But like I said, I think I have an inkling of who may have taken her. You just need to watch my memory first."

Parker nodded. "Come on, then. We're wasting time... can I—get my gun?" He looked over his shoulder at it laying on the dusty floor.

"As long as you don't plan on using it on me or Carrie." Greysen's cadence sounded playful, but there was a hint of seriousness in his words as well.

"They don't need guns, Price. They have a car," Carrie said through clenched teeth.

Parker looked over at Noriana at that statement, who brandished a hidden smirk. She must have thought Carrie was a bad guy.

She'd been protecting him.

She was fearless.

As long as he could have her by his side, he was safe.

SIXTEEN

PARKER

Parker stood face-to-face with the woman in the gold cat-eye glasses and the professional suit, the one who had locked him in the conference room before.

"Uh, excuse me!" She stood from her seat, though when she saw Greysen behind Parker, she slowly sat back down, nodding to him. She pressed her nose into her planner and looked over each of them carefully as they passed by. Her eyes hardened when they came to Parker.

He wanted to be a smart ass and throw her the bird. But there were more important things to worry about. And granted, she'd just been doing her job earlier.

Parker followed behind until they'd passed all the cubicles and came to a room in the back of the building.

Greysen typed a code into the keypad, pressed his thumb print down on the pad, and the door unlocked. He opened it, allowing Carrie, Noriana, and Parker to enter, then stepping in himself.

The room wasn't particularly large, and a reclining chair sat in the middle with a computer on a rolling cart next to it. The room was quite sterile, smelling of antiseptic. Parker hated it.

The smell and the equipment brought him back to the room he'd experienced hell in. Of course, lots of the equipment had been updated since the last time he'd been in the same room as the Memory Machine. The most intriguing update was the fact the chair bore no restraints now. Perhaps because most people now experiencing *going under* with this new prototype did so voluntarily, as opposed to how the other one had been abused.

Or perhaps this one allowed you more control of your outer body during the 'procedure'. Both thoughts were chilling.

"Why does it need to be so... medical?" Parker asked, watching Noriana soak in the room. It seemed as though she was in a daze.

"Medical? Never thought of it that way," Carrie answered.

Greysen and Carrie had gone straight to work once the door was closed. Crinkling open tools from wrappers and untangling wires. Greysen typed vigorously into the computer, pulling up files and charts and graphs—stuff that looked like another language to Parker.

Parker seized the opportunity to sit Nori down on a folding chair by the counter behind the Memory Machine.

He pulled her head back gently and looked at the wound on her forehead. It was pretty deep. He wasn't entirely sure if she'd need stitches or not. "How are you feeling?" he asked her gently.

She nodded. "I'm okay, Parker. All this stuff... this is weird," she whispered to him.

He smiled. "It's surreal right? Like spy movie shit?"

She nodded again.

"Are you feeling light-headed or dizzy at all?"

She shook her head.

"I'm just making sure you didn't get a concussion when you crashed the car. Can I clean your head?" He moved a piece of her hair off to the side of her face, trailing his finger gently down her cheek.

She nodded.

He'd never witnessed her this quiet before. She was out of her element. He couldn't tell what she was thinking based on her body language. Parker leaned over and wet a clean towel he'd found on the counter with warm water in the sink. He turned and looked at Carrie and Greysen, who were both fully concentrated on what they were working on.

Nerds, tapping into the computer system and memory machine.

He turned back to Nori and began to gently dab the warm washcloth by her chin and up the side of her face, clearing away blood that had dried. Periodically, he'd reach over and rinse it in the sink, then return to her with a clean edge. When he got to her forehead, he parted her hair, cleaning as close to the wound as he could get without her wincing. "You might need stitches. You got it good," he whispered.

She opened her mouth.

"Don't worry—I'm not going to do them. I may have learned a thing or two from Stephen, but I'm not into needles."

"Not into needles?" Carrie called out from across the room. "Well this should be interesting," she said to Greysen.

Parker sighed. He'd forgotten about the IV serum. *Frick.* What was he doing? Why couldn't

Greysen just tell him what had happened? Why did he have to *show* him?

Perhaps so he could see the truth for himself and know Greysen wasn't just making stuff up? That was a good enough reason, Parker supposed.

"Bandages?" Parker asked, ignoring Carrie's comment.

"Second drawer from the left," Greysen called out over his shoulder.

Parker pulled open the drawer to find all different sorts of bandages. He grabbed a few tiny butterfly ones. "So do you have a room like this in all the Humavision buildings?" He bit his lip as he closed the drawer.

Carrie spoke up again over her shoulder. "Of course. First-aid is necessary in our production departments. In most companies they just have an eye-washing station or something, but we went all out. It's proven useful."

Parker nodded and then turned to Noriana with an alcohol pad in his hand. "You want to do this yourself? You have to clean it before I can put these bandages on it. These will hold it together until we can get somewhere where you can get stitches."

Nori looked at him, her gaze wavering, and took the alcohol pad. She turned from him as she swiped it across the wound a few times, wincing while doing it. She tossed the bloodied pad onto the counter next to them with glistening eyes.

"I'm so sorry, babe," he whispered again.

She shook her head. "It's nothing."

"You ready?" Greysen asked over his shoulder.

"Yeah, just a sec." Parker carefully placed the three bandages across Noriana's wound, and, desperately wanting to kiss her, held his desires in check as he instead turned to face Greysen and Carrie.

He pushed off the chair and walked over to them, sitting up on the leather reclining chair. Metal jabbed into his lower back, and he leaned forward and pulled out the gun that had been in the back of his pants. He held it up a moment and shrugged.

Noriana stood and joined him at the chair. She took the gun and placed it on the counter behind her, then grabbed Parker's hand.

"Let's just get it over with, okay?" Parker muttered. "Every moment spent in here is another of my mom being gone. If this will help, let's get the show on the road." His heart pounded in his chest. He watched as Greysen walked over to Noriana. He took his own gun out.

Parker tensed as Noriana squeezed his hand tighter. But then Greysen set his gun next to Parker's on the counter, and he let go of all muscle tightening, leaning his head back on the chair.

Carrie lifted the headgear with wires protruding from it up and onto Parker's head. It settled snug around his skull. Where the metal trackers were placed, it was cold on his scalp.

He watched Carrie ready the IV. She took his arm and rubbed some gel on the inside crease. "What's that?" he asked, the sensation cool on his skin. He'd never seen them use that before. His arm tingled for a moment before he couldn't feel anything in that area.

"It's a gentle, topical anesthetic. Numbs the area. You don't like needles, so I thought you'd appreciate it."

He nodded, giving a small half-smile. Everything was all happening so fast.

Greysen approached the chair next to Nori, looking first at the screen and then at Parker, white as a ghost. "Parker," he breathed. "You have the ability to pull out of the scene at any time that you'd like. I would recommend, however, even if you are feeling strong psychological impulses to the information you are receiving from my memory, that you allow it to play out until it's finished, so that you don't miss any pieces or have any misunderstandings of what you see."

All of this was too much. His knees were weak, and he concentrated deeply on steadying his hands from trembling. Parker's heart raced, and he had no idea what Greysen needed so badly for him to see. Yes, he was about to find out, but the anticipation was murder. "Okay, got it." He looked away from Carrie as he saw a glimpse of the shiny metal skewer she was going to poke him with. Even if he could no longer feel it, he couldn't bear watch it go in, right in front of him. He looked over to his fiancé. He was glad she was here. Time and time again.

It happened faster than he'd imagined. Because he wasn't looking, he didn't feel the pinch of the needle piercing his skin. Or the rush of burning liquid entering his veins from the serum bag that hung from the rolling IV stand next to Carrie. But he did feel that sickly feeling, the one you feel right when you're taken from your comfortable level of consciousness. It pulled him, and he let go. He let go of all resistance, for fear that he'd get stuck between the worlds, one of his biggest nightmares. And at first, everything was black.

So much darkness.

But then... a scene opened up before him.

The ring of a loud bell rang out behind him, and he was spun around inside Greysen's perspective, to see a large brick building, *a school*, a high school, with students running every which way: up the stairs into the building, leaning against cars, playing football in the yard. It was like a movie, only Parker was a character in it.

Someone quickly moved past him, a stack of books in their arms. This was surreal. He wasn't prepared for what he saw next.

His eyes locked on a girl walking towards him. She had long brown hair with a ribbon headband. He'd seen that girl in photos. He'd seen similar features in himself when he looked in the mirror.

His mom. As a teenager. And she walked towards him. Only he had to keep remembering it wasn't him.

Greysen. She was walking toward Greysen.
What the hell...

This was just beyond weird.

Parker had never known what Greysen looked like when he was younger, except from the photo he'd seen recently in that yearbook.

And it was suddenly clear to Parker that the thing Greysen was so nervous about, and so desperately wanted him to understand, had something to do with his mom's relationship with Greysen back when they were in high school. That made him nervous. Nervous only until his emotions and feelings were clouded and faint, and he took on the emotions of the memory he was in.

He felt a strong sense of desire, almost to the point of jealousy. *Control.* And then, as his mom walked up to Greysen and hugged him, the strongest emotion of all took over his entire body. Warmth. A tingling longing.

Love.

Love? *Holy shit.* Greysen hadn't just *known* his mom. Hadn't just had a relationship with her. He'd *loved* her.

Granted, they'd been teenagers. And this kind of strong love and desire that surged through his body now, it wasn't the same kind of feeling he had for Nori. It was different.

 Lustful. Immature.

Parker squirmed underneath the forced upon emotions. Even a memory machine's influence wasn't enough to cover up all the awkward that coursed through his veins. His attention was directed back to the conversation at hand.

"Dottie, what's up? You said you needed to talk?" Greysen asked, releasing the hug with his hands on her hips.

She backed away from his grasp, and Parker felt Greysen's emotions tangle. He was confused.

"I *told* you we shouldn't have done that, that one night," she mumbled, her head down.

"Why? That was the best night of my life."

Oh god. Parker did *not* want to think about what they were referring to. This was his *mom*. His mom didn't have sex. Sex and his mom did *not* belong in the same sentence together, the same thought. *No. No. No.*

"Grey, I'm..." She held her hand over her stomach. "I'm pregnant."

Greysen staggered backwards.

Parker was overcome with an overwhelming panic. *What?* Suddenly, dates flooded his mind and he tried to do the math, but he didn't know exactly what year they were in here. He couldn't remember the class year on the spine of the yearbook. He didn't know if this was the same year as those pictures were taken, anyway. He was the oldest child in his family. How old was he, even!? He couldn't think, couldn't concentrate, because all of his thoughts and emotions were suppressed from the memory, and all he felt now was what Greysen had felt then.

Overwhelmed. Terrified. Excited?

"Mine?" Greysen whispered.

Dottie crossed her arms and backed up again. "You think I'm a put-out or something?"

"No. Oh my god. Dot, we can... we can do this. Okay..." Parker was forced into a pace in front of her. He lifted his head, a smile forcing on his lips. He placed his hands on either side of her shoulders. "We can do this! I... Dottie, I haven't said this before, but—I love you."

She moved her hand up to her mouth, eyes beginning to water. "Grey, don't. I'm not... I'm not keeping it," she said softly.

Parker's throat constricted. He continued to try to do the math in his head.

"What? Why? You can't... it's a baby. You're going to get an abortion?"

She looked down. "I can't have a baby, Greysen. Not now, not with..."

"With me. Is that it? You can't have a baby with me?" Greysen let go of her shoulders and turned from her. Parker's view of her was whiplashed to the side as Greysen turned his head.

Anger clouded Parker's judgement as he watched. *No, experienced.*

He heard Dottie sniffling and crying. She spoke, "What about college? You're too smart not to go on and be some big inventor, helping the world. You don't need something you did in your teen years to hold you back! And me? What about me? It's my body, and my decision. We have a choice in this. It's still so early."

"Can I think about this?" Parker almost got dizzy as Greysen spun back to face her. "Please. Dottie, please," Greysen begged breathlessly, and to Parker's shock, he dropped down to his knees in front of her. "Don't do anything just yet. Can we think about it?"

Dottie grabbed his hands, bringing him to his feet. The crease between her eyes told Parker she was also angry. He'd seen that line only a few times in his life, when he and his brothers really wore on her nerves. It softened as she looked into his face. *Greysen's* face. The bell on the building rang again. She glanced over Greysen's shoulder. "We have to go," she said softly. "I'll... just a little bit of time," she answered.

Greysen nodded vigorously.

"I'll see you," she sang regretfully, turning on her heel and heading back down the hill towards the building, along with a few other stragglers who rushed into the building at the sound of the late bell.

Greysen turned and butted his back against the tree, then slid down to ground, hugging his knees.

Parker felt the weight of the situation bearing down on him. So heavy, so hard to carry.

Greysen's eyes poured tears, a headache sharpening at his temples. His shoulders bent over and shook.

The feeling of defeat was so intense, Parker felt the urge to get out. He wanted out. He wanted that feeling to be powerful enough to signal the outside.

And sure enough, a sickly, spinning feeling erupted in his head, and the world went dark. He didn't swirl into another memory, it was just darkness. Until he began to hear a sound at the other end of the tunnel.

Parker?

It was his name. Being called.

"Parker?" It was stronger this time.

It all flooded back to him. He blinked his eyes open, trying to sit up.

"Easy, easy." Carrie's voice carried through as she pushed his shoulder back on the chair.

He reached up. "My head..." The headgear had been removed. He looked around the room as his blurred vision came into focus. He was still in the office room they'd set up in. He looked

232

around at all the faces, Noriana standing next to him with worried panic across her face. Carrie typed vigorously into the computer, printing off scans.

Parker hadn't even noticed her remove the IV from his arm, placing a cotton ball and bandage in the crook of his elbow.

Then he looked at Greysen.

Across the room.

Emotions tore away at him. Over what he'd just seen. What he'd just experienced.

What am I feeling? It was so confusing, and it felt his brain had a hard time catching up with his raging emotions. The first feeling, though, the strongest one, was confusion.

"You're..." His voice came out a croak, and Parker paused, swallowing hard. "Greysen," he tried again, "are you... are you my...?" Parker couldn't even voice the words because he didn't believe them. Voicing those words would mean he didn't know who he was. That his whole world was not what he'd thought it was. That he was someone entirely different. His throat swelled, not allowing him to speak.

"What's going on?" Noriana butted in-between them and placed her hand on Parker's chest. "Parker, are you okay?"

"He should be regaining feeling in his legs here soon," Carrie offered helpfully, still staring at the computer screen and fully in work mode.

Nori interrupted her. "Not physically, Genius! Can't you see what's going on here?!" She lowered her gaze from Carrie back to Parker. "What happened, Parker? What did you see? You're white as a ghost!"

Parker shook his head. This was too much to process.

Though the next emotion to emerge was clearer than any of his previous feelings.

It was deep. Like a dark cloud.

Betrayal.

Betrayed by his parents.

Betrayed by his entire existence.

And most of all... betrayed by Greysen.

Parker moved to get up off the chair.

"Slow down, you're going to feel really weak—" Carrie started.

He didn't care. He pushed off the chair, anyway. Noriana reached for his hand and he yanked it away, keeping his eyes on Greysen. "This whole time," he snarled. "In Paris... you knew exactly what you were doing. How could you?" He narrowed his eyes, anger seething through his blood. Heat engulfed his vision, his thoughts.

Greysen advanced toward him. "Parker. You were going to find out sooner or later. And I think you knowing can help us—"

Parker turned from Greysen and marched for the door.

Greysen reached out to grab his arm and Parker jerked backwards out of his grasp, adrenaline pumping. *"Don't* touch me!" He yanked the door open and slammed it behind him, leaving the three others, including Noriana, in his wake.

His vision was still a tad blurry, mostly from his fit of rage as opposed to any physiological effect of the memory procedure. He heard Greysen say to Nori through the door, "You best give him some space."

Parker couldn't organize his thoughts. He barreled through the halls, forgetting how they'd come through here. Nothing rang a bell from the last time he'd been here only hours ago because before, he had exited through the ceiling.

Eventually, he found an exit door and pushed out of it, into the outside. He took a big breath of air into his lungs, then hunched over, his hands on his knees, and let it go.

Dramatic, heaving sobs racked his body. He pressed his back against the building and sunk to the ground, knees up.

Greysen is my father?

How could his mom keep this secret from him his whole life? How could his parents lead him to believe that he was fully theirs? That he was fully related to his brothers? That another piece of him wasn't living out there, somewhere? Was there ever a plan to tell him? Did they think he'd never find out?

He was already twenty-eight. He'd lived twenty-eight years not knowing the truth of where he came from.

Did this sudden revelation really change anything?

Just because he came from Greysen, didn't mean Greysen was his father. His *dad* was his father. Davis Rubec. He'd raised Parker. Loved him.

Did his parents know about Greysen finding him in Paris, and working with him in Chicago? Did his mom know that Grice from the bestseller he'd written was, in fact, the Greysen she'd conceived Parker with?

He had so many questions.

Why now? Why is Greysen bringing this up now? He's had so many opportunities before. Why choose this time? Because Mom is missing?

He pulled out his phone and dialed.

"Hello?"

"Stephen. There's an old warehouse in the West Bottoms, off Twelfth Street. Double doors, grand staircase. Chess-like-looking pieces on the roof trim. You know it?"

"I know the area. Parker, are you okay?"

"Take the PI there. I think Mom was held there. She's not there now, that I know of, but there's evidence people just left. Go quickly."

"Roger. How'd you kn—nevermind. I'll let you know what happens."

"Bye." Parker hung up and pocketed his phone, a major headache erupting at the base of his skull.

Stephen was potentially his half-brother.

Parker had so much to think about. So much to go over. He sat against the building, suffocated by his thoughts and feelings and wanting nothing more than to crawl into a hole and never resurface.

After a while, the door he'd escaped out of burst open.

He looked up from his tear-smeared palms to see Noriana standing there, looking around until her eyes landed on him. She knelt down and grabbed his hands.

"Where do I even go from here?" he asked weakly.

237

"I... I don't know. I can't imagine how you're feeling," she said with a pained sigh. "Parker, despite everything, your mom is still missing, yes? So why don't we focus on that? And maybe you can ask her for answers when we find her?"

He nodded, leaning forward and wrapping his arms around her for a hug.

"What was that thing like?" she asked quietly into his ear. "I've never seen anything like it."

"The memory machine?"

She nodded.

"It was... I don't know. I never want to do it again, though. I think it's best we stay out of other people's thoughts and memories. It could be really dangerous. Plus, I was so overcome by Greysen's emotions because it was *his* memory. It was entirely biased. I don't know any information except that one side."

"So there you go," she said quietly.

"Hm?" he asked, looking up.

"You said it yourself. It's one-sided. So you need to get your mom's side of the story, too."

He nodded. "You're right... it's just so hard. I don't even know who I am anymore. What's real and what's not." His neck slumped forward. It was as though sand filled his limbs.

"You are strong, Parker." She lifted his chin gently with her fingers. "You're funny. And sweet.

And caring. You are who you are. Don't doubt that."

"Thank you. I love you." His appreciation was a little weak, but he was grateful for her.

"Parker, take your time and when you're ready, we can leave together, okay?" She stood and reached for the door.

"Nori?"

"Hm?"

He looked up at her. "Can you just stay with me for a little while longer?"

Without a response, she sat back down on the pavement next to him and laid her head on his shoulder.

Parker heaved a long, weighted sigh. If he could have this moment for just a little while longer, this bubble that surrounded them which no one could penetrate, then maybe he could catch his breath enough to face his truth.

SEVENTEEN

GREYSEN

G reysen plopped into a fold-out chair and rested his head in his hands. His yanked his hair a moment and then looked up at Carrie, who stood awkwardly by the computer, wide-eyed. He sighed and shook his head. "That did not go as planned."

"Do you want me to—I just... Greysen, how can I help you?" she asked, taking a step toward him and then stopping.

He looked up at her again. Battered and bruised. She'd helped him through everything. For goodness sake, she'd just been hit by a car an hour or so ago. "I'm so sorry you've been dragged through all of this. You shouldn't be here." He stood and began to pace. A nervous tick.

"Are you firing me?" she whimpered, then pushed her glasses back up on her nose.

"No! No, definitely not. I mean, I'd be happy if you *wanted* to stay. In fact, you deserve a raise. A bonus. I'm going to give you a bonus when we get back to Chicago." He half expected her to be happy about that, but she didn't smile or express gratitude.

She just stood there, a serious look on her face. "With the money in your trunk?"

The question hit him like a bag of bricks. He'd completely forgotten about that in his rush to catch up to Parker and explain everything. "I..." He went to the counter and leaned against it. "I was only instructed to bring it here. Nothing else. I don't know what to do with it now. I mean, I guess I figured they'd approach me again at some point and give me the next step."

"So we're being controlled by gang bangers now?" Her inflection grim.

He straightened up, looked her dead on, and shrugged.

She walked up to him. "Is that what you want? Is that how you want to conduct business?"

A red flag went up in his mind. He cocked an eyebrow and took a step back. Where was this coming from? Had Carrie known more about the shady operation going on at Humavision than she'd led on during the car ride?

He panicked a little, looking back and forth around the room before his eyes landed on her again. "No, it's not. I don't want anything to do with this."

"Then why are you letting it happen? I know you, Greysen Price. As your assistant, I've studied you. You drink one cup of coffee in the morning. You always grab two packets of sugar, but you only put one in. The other one goes in a drawer in your office for God knows what reason. You are an honest man. You don't take shit from anyone. You've let the fear of losing power when you've finally got power go straight to your head, and let me tell you..."

Greysen froze. He'd pressed himself up against the counter, as far away as he could get from her. His heart pounded in his chest.

Carrie continued. "...you are a far better man than Edrick Crowder ever was. You do not have to do this." She took one more look at him, then shook her head and turned away.

All suspicion of Carrie having anything to do with the mysterious duffle bag of money had been swept aside. She was trying to help him. And she was right.

Carrie was a wake-up call. And one who believed in him more than he deserved.

"You're right," he whispered. "What do I do?"

"You'll figure it out." She half-smiled, walking to the door. "I need a drink of water. I'll be back." She opened the door.

"Carrie?"

She looked back over her shoulder.

"The other sugar is for my three o'clock coffee. So I don't have to go back down to the breakroom."

She smiled. "Still makes no sense." Then she closed the door and left him to the empty room.

EIGHTEEN

PARKER

Parker had just wondered how long it'd take Stephen and the PI to find any more information on the mattress and handcuff scene at the old Humavision warehouse in the West Bottoms when his phone vibrated in his pocket. He wrestled it out and hit the answer button. "Hello?"

"Parker, we found her."

His whole world blackened around his vision as his mind caught up with what he'd just heard, and everything collapsed around him. He pushed up from the ground, away from Noriana's grasp.

He'd waited so long to hear those words, never knowing if he'd ever hear them. He dropped the phone by his side, bending to his knees and heaving a large breath. Then the terror followed, and he brought the phone back to his ear as the words vomited from his mouth before he had time to catch them: "Is she alive?"

The hesitation from the receiver was physically painful. But then Stephen spoke clearly, "Goddamn Parker, yes. Yes, she's alive." His voice wavered. "And you're gonna want to come home as quick as possible."

"She's home?"

"Yeah."

"Okay, okay I'm on my way." He hung up before Stephen had the chance to say anything else. Though there was something in his brother's voice that wasn't quite right. Parker had caught that inflection at the beginning of the call, only he'd misinterpreted it for bad news. In reality, the news was better than he could have hoped for. Better than he'd imagined, his worry spiraling out of control as days and days passed since Stephen had first called him in Paris to tell him she'd gone missing.

Parker wanted to be happy about the phone call, but something was just wrong.

"What is it?" Nori asked, grabbing his arm once more.

"We have to go." His eyes locked onto hers. "They found her."

She inhaled, her eyes bearing a look of concern, and turned to open the door for him.

Parker barreled through, heading back for the building entrance.

"Parker?"

He turned to see Carrie at the water cooler, filling up her water bottle.

She looked like a deer in the headlights as she looked up at him. "You're leaving?"

"Tell Greysen they found her. Tell him... he's lucky." Parker turned to Nori. "It'd probably be better if you drove. Stephen's car is in the lot," he said quietly to her, and she nodded, taking lead.

Noriana pulled into the driveway of his parents' home in the Northland of Kansas City, and Parker leapt out of the passenger side door before she'd even switched the gear into park.

Stephen stood on the porch, waiting.

Parker tore for the house.

But his brother hurried down the stairs and stopped him by holding out an arm, urging him back.

"Is she in there?" Parker demanded.

Stephen nodded, putting a hand against Parker's chest to hold him at bay. "But I feel you need to hear this first before you see her."

"What? What happened? Is she okay? Did someone hurt her?" Parker had already thought of all the possibilities. Had something happened to her face that Stephen wanted to warn him about before he saw her? Stephen was an ER doctor. He saw the worst of the worst. Was this even bad for him to see?

"Parker." Stephen looked down and closed his eyes, then shook his head a moment before lifting his gaze back to Parker. "She... she left of her own accord. You know Mom's always been a free spirit. She needed to get away."

Parker heard the words come out of his brother's mouth in slow motion. *No. No way.* His thoughts jumbled and he was dumbfounded. *Left on her own?* His cheeks burned. He scratched the back of his neck and looked over his shoulder. *Where's Nori?* His throat was suddenly so dry he couldn't swallow. "What? C'mon, that can't be true..." When the realization of his brother's words absorbed through his disbelief, a fire emerged in his gut and worked its way up. Parker placed his hand on his stomach, nauseous. Just when he went to lean over, someone came through the front door behind Stephen.

Their mom.

"Parker... don't get upset now." She moved to the front porch, squinting down at them in the grass. She wore a flowing dress, her skin bearing a new glow to it. She'd gone somewhere warm.

248

"Don't—" he laughed out loud. "Don't get upset?" Parker barely noticed as Stephen motioned for Noriana to join him in the house. They stepped inside, skirting around Parker and his mom, leaving them alone to talk.

Everything around him was a blur. It was better that way. Nori was there to support him, but right now he really needed some alone time with his mom.

"It was all a misunderstanding," his mom said as soon as the door had shut behind Nori and Stephen. She raised her hands up and shrugged her shoulders.

"How so?" Parker asked. *Do I want to know?*

No. Instinct told him to leave and go crawl in a hole again. Allow himself to absorb this new discovery and catch up before he unleashed any initial reactions. Especially any he might regret. He didn't know what to think or what to say. He didn't know who he was or where he came from anymore.

She moved a step closer, and he moved a step back. The last thing he wanted right now was for her to be closer. He furrowed his brow. His breath labored.

Her facial expression dropped, color draining from her face, probably the moment she realized this was more serious than she'd thought. She rubbed her arm and shifted her weight from one foot to the other. Then, she continued, "I had to get away. Not—not like a housewife get-away. People were coming around here and asking questions about you and your involvement with... I had to make it look like I was gone until the coast was clear. I don't even know if the coast is clear now, really. But your dad said it was getting bad here, that people were getting really worried."

"Dad knew?" His stomach flipped. Now he had so many more questions. Where to even begin? She had no idea what he knew, and he had no idea what she might be implying. "Mom," he said finally, "I know about Greysen Price... and you." The back of his neck burned.

Her arms dropped to her side, dangling helplessly.

"The person coming and asking questions," he pressed on, "did it have anything to do with Greysen, or with Humavision?" This time, he moved closer to her. He saw the curtains move in the family room window.

Stephen, probably making sure they were still alive out here.

She nodded, looking away from his gaze.

"Who came here to question you?" he urged. A weight lifted off his conscious that he'd at least been correct about the connection.

She was quiet a moment.

"I know more than you think." His voice came out lower than he'd expected when he spoke. He narrowed his gaze.

Just as she parted her lips to speak, the rev of a car engine pulled up to the curb behind him.

"Oh hell no." Parker turned as Greysen pushed out of the driver's seat and waved the man away, pointing back down the road. At least Carrie hadn't come, too. Greysen must have left to follow him and Nori right after they'd left the Humavision building. "You are not welcome here. Go!" he yelled through gritted teeth.

"Parker!" Dottie reprimanded.

"No. We're not doing this—" He pointed at his mom, then back to Greysen. "—right now." He shook his head. His heart beat fast in his chest.

Greysen put his hands up in surrender. "I know you're upset, Parker—"

"No," Parker repeated, biting off the word. "You don't get to speak to me like that." He felt like the pickle in the middle, bouncing back and forth between two liars.

But then, Greysen and Dottie caught sight of each other, and it was as though the whole world melted away around them. Parker felt involuntarily pushed to the background, a spectator in his own story. He'd never seen Greysen's face the way it looked now.

The man walked up to Parker's mom, but not too close. "I haven't... I haven't seen you in a long time," he croaked. "I mean, I've seen you in *him*— he has your mannerisms. He's all you, Dot." Greysen's eyes glistened as he stared at Dottie. He stood rigid in place.

He's talking about me? Parker placed his hand on his stomach, sickened. The lie continued, only out in the open now.

She didn't seem like she was trying to shield this news from Parker, though, unless she thought Greysen was speaking cryptically enough.

And then he thought about his dad, who was just inside the house. Or, the guy who'd raised him was just inside the house. Parker knew him as Dad, but he wasn't biologically Dad? The man in the house had known that his wife had gone to a beach to disappear for a while. He'd played the part that she had been kidnapped. He was also a good liar. *Had he known that Parker wasn't his? He had to have known.*

Should I allow them this moment? He didn't want to. He didn't think they deserved it. But then... he thought of the memory he'd experienced. Greysen's memory of Dottie by the tree. The pained feeling Parker had felt in Greysen that that was one of the last times he'd seen her. Because shortly after that, she'd taken off. Moved away. That free spirit Stephen had mentioned.

Everything sounded so familiar.

Parker was just like her. He'd harnessed his mom's free spirit when he'd dropped everything and went to Paris on a whim.

Because of the memory he'd witnessed, Parker decided he would allow them this moment.

"I never had closure, Dottie," Greysen finally said softly.

"I'm sorry," she nearly whispered, her voice cracking. She stole a glance toward the house before looking back at Greysen. "I had to leave. Everything was so overwhelming, and I wanted... well I didn't know what I wanted, Grey. We were kids."

Parker shuddered at the mention of Greysen's nickname again.

"I got scared when people came questioning about..." She touched her collarbone.

"The locket," Greysen mouthed.

"The locket?" Parker asked.

Greysen looked past Parker, fixated on Dottie. "Do you still have it?" His eyes were as round as saucers. His hand trembled by his side.

She shook her head. "I lost it. I brought it with me to Cabo... I was on a boat and I leaned over." She paused and avoided his gaze. "It fell in the ocean, Grey. I'm sorry. I know it was important to you."

Greysen's shoulders slumped again. The color drained from his face.

"But I guess it's a good thing because then she couldn't take it from me. I'm not sure her intentions were noble. Actually, she was quite aggressive. That's when I knew I was in trouble. *You* were in trouble, and they were coming for me, regardless of the fact I told her we hadn't been in contact for a long time."

"Who?" Greysen pressed. "Who's *she?*"

"A woman named Molly Green."

Parker stood a step back. He'd never thought he'd hear that name on his mom's lips. He looked over at Greysen to see the man's face had gone even more pale, if possible.

Greysen turned to pace a moment, but then looked back.

Dottie spoke first. "Why does this...Molly person want that locket? Why did she come here, Greysen? To *me*, of all people?"

Greysen reached up and put his fingers in the hair he had left, yanking it a moment before releasing it. He whispered gruffly. "It wasn't just a locket, Dot. It holds a computer chip in it... I didn't tell you before because I didn't want you to freak out. But the chip has some vital information on it. An invention prototype that cannot get into the wrong hands." He scratched his head. "I didn't... I didn't think anyone would make the connection between us. I never would have sent it if I knew it'd bring you danger," he pleaded.

Parker parted his lips to speak, but then closed them again. He raised an eyebrow. *What? He's never said anything about a chip the entire time I've known him. What else did he leave out of his story?* Parker stretched his neck from side to side and balled his fists at his sides until his knuckles whitened. His breaths came up short again.

The lies and deceit continued.

Dottie shifted again, as though she were uncomfortable. She turned to her son. "Parker, maybe you should go inside and join the others while I say goodbye here to our friend."

Our friend? "I'm not going anywhere. I still have questions!"

"Parker..." she breathed, annoyance on her face.

255

"I told you, I know about you and Greysen."

"Yes sweetie, we've known each other since we were kids."

"No, Dottie, he *knows*," Greysen said, dragging that last word out, sincerity on his face.

Balled-up emotion tried to force its way out of Parker's body. He squirmed.

His mom just stood there, as if waiting for further explanation. She seemed confused.

Greysen stepped toward her. "I had always kind of followed him growing up from a distance, since you took that away from me, but when I was finally able to come face-to-face with him in Paris, even though he didn't know who I was, I felt as though it was better that I wasn't involved in his upbringing, after all."

Parker brought his hand to his stomach again. It swirled with nerves. *I'm gonna be sick...*

"Involved in his up—what are you going on about?" Dottie raised her voice. "I am sincerely confused!" She put her hand on her hip.

"Don't try and hide it anymore, Mom," Parker muttered. He scrubbed a hand over his eyes, exhausted by all of this. "It's maddening."

"Dot," Greysen replied softly. "He's our son."

Her face drained of its color. "Our son? Is that what you...?" She shook her head. "Parker is not *our* son. He's not... he's not the baby we

256

conceived. I'm so sorry if that's what you thought this   whole   time."

"I want a DNA test." Greysen spat.

"No, Grey...Parker was conceived by me and his father, who's—" she turned halfway to the house, "his father is inside."

Greysen went rigid.

Parker froze. His vision tunneled first to his mom, then to Greysen. *Wait... Greysen was wrong? He led me to believe he was my father...* Greysen had stalked him. Pursued him. For nothing? For a boy that wasn't his own?

Greysen nearly fell to his knees, but staggered, then caught himself against the trunk of Stephen's car. "What about the baby we...?" His voice cracked.

"Oh Grey, I'm so sorry. I had a miscarriage shortly after I told you about it."

Greysen did hit his knees then, tears streaking down his cheeks. "But... you... you left. How was I supposed to... Why didn't you tell me?"

Dottie dropped to her knees as well in front of him.

Parker squirmed again, scrunching up his face. *I shouldn't be here...* All the implications of their reunion were resurfacing in front of him, and it wasn't really his business. Not anymore. His mom looked as though she were afraid to touch

Greysen. Parker stepped back from them, but couldn't tear his eyes away.

"I have... never told that to anyone," she cracked, now also crying on the front lawn. "Even though I had this full life with a beautiful family and a husband." She looked over her shoulder at the house again. "I love them all very much, but I'll never forget the loss I had when I was a kid myself. I wasn't able to tell anyone at the time." She smeared both her eyes with her hand. "I had lived with the loss alone. And then... and then I met Davis. And we fell hard for one another. And he gave me Parker." She nodded over toward him, then rose to her feet and walked to him. "Oh, my baby boy." She put the palms of her hands on his cheeks. "Were you thinking this whole time I had lied to you about who your dad was? I'm so sorry you felt that way." She threw her arms around him.

He felt heavy. Words did not come easy. He had a knot in his throat. "I'm sorry, Mom," he whispered in her ear and he hugged her tightly. "I didn't know you'd been through that."

"Oh honey." Her voice wavered. "I'm sorry for all this trouble." She turned again to Greysen, her arm still around Parker.

Greysen was gutted. He stood, but just barely. His hand on his stomach, he looked as though

258

he'd aged twenty years. "I have to... I'm sorry, I have to go. I just don't know what to—I'm sorry," he stuttered, moving backwards to his car.

Parker advanced forward. "You okay to drive right now?" For some reason, he now felt massive empathy for this man. Perhaps because even as Parker's life was being mended back together with the truth, Greysen's world must have been deteriorating with that same truth.

Parker would try to find him later to check on him, after his family, his true family, mended what had happened here today on the lawn.

But Parker imagined that this day would not be one of the memories Greysen would want to retrieve using the memory machine ever again.

NINETEEN

GREYSEN

Greysen's hands were numb on steering wheel. He drove away from the Rubec's house on autopilot. He just wanted to get far, far away. As fast as he could with blurry vision and a broken heart. He drove and drove until he reached downtown. There was a spot he'd used to visit all the time in Kansas City when he would come back for business trips.

The WWI Memorial.

Back in the day, he'd run the stairs at the memorial for exercise. And at the top, there was a tower that rose to the sky and had a real torch at the top; it's fire could be seen from a distance. When he'd walk up to the wall adjacent to the tower and look over it, he'd be confronted with a beautiful view of the entire city, with Union Station at its forefront. This place had been a haven of reflection for him in the past, and it was the only place he could think of to go to right now. So he cleared his mind the best he could and drove until he got there.

He parked the car, not remembering the drive, and got out, pacing the walk.

Whereas he'd been ready to aid Parker in picking up the pieces of his life as he knew it, and to help him learn who he truly was, there was nobody here to do that for Greysen. Nobody who could possibly understand.

Parker was not his son.

Never was.

He walked up the stairs to the Memorial, his legs weak, his lungs small. He reached the wall that overlooked Union Station with the cityscape behind it and leaned against it.

The stone wall supported him as he reflected on his actual child, the one Dottie had told him about back when they were just teenagers, the one who had passed away before they were even born.

It was as though Greysen now felt the loss of two children.

The one who had never come to be, and the one who was never his to begin with.

Being a dad just wasn't in the cards for him, it seemed. It was probably better off that way.

He heaved a weighted sigh. To think he'd never have any sort of legacy. That Humavision, a company he didn't even have full control over, when all he did was fight for control, would be the only thing he'd leave behind when he died.

Then it hit him. The money in his trunk.

Why did he feel like he didn't have control?

Because someone else held all the cards.

This entire time he'd been looking in the wrong direction.

But the Rubecs had pointed him to the true man in charge of his destiny without even knowing. The one who was always one step ahead of him, holding the cards.

This person had beaten him to Dottie in search of the locket. A locket that had now been lost to the depths forever. *It was better that way anyhow...*

But this person... was Molly.

There was no other explanation for it.

Molly could be anywhere now. If she'd come to visit Dottie before Dot had gone missing, then she'd have been here maybe only three or so days ago. There was still a chance she could be in the city. And that shady messenger had told Greysen to bring the money to Kansas City with him.

She was here. She had to still be here.

263

Greysen trekked back to the car, nodding at a guy wearing workout clothes as he passed him. When he got back to the car, he went to the trunk. He'd suddenly had more energy as he inserted the key.

But when he lifted the trunk door and peered inside, his heart sank.

The duffle bag was gone.

Shit!

He was always a step behind her.

Greysen slammed the trunk in a rage and put his head down, scowling the whole way to the driver's seat. He shimmied his phone out of his pocket and dialed.

Carrie picked up faster than he'd have guessed. "Carrie, are you still at IT?" He put his keys in the ignition but sat in park.

"Yes." It was as though her answer jumped on his question.

"They took it. They took the money." He was out of breath. He held the phone back from his face so she couldn't hear him panting. The nerves built in his stomach.

"I know," she said quickly.

Greysen cocked his brow. It was then he heard someone mumbling in the background of Carrie's line.

"Can you come here—back to the IT building?" she asked, her tone an octave higher than normal.

"Carrie, are you okay?" He pulled the phone back and looked at its face a moment before smashing it back to his ear. "Oh my god, someone's there controlling what you say, aren't they? Carrie, hand them the phone. I want to talk to those fu—"

The line went dead.

They hung up on me!

Greysen patted all around his waist. His stomach sunk. *My gun!* He rushed around to the driver side door and swung it open, leaning inside. He threw open the glove compartment. *Nothing.* Under the seat? *Nothing.*

And then it hit him. *I set the gun down next to Parker's at the IT building, right before the memory machine. Shit.*

His nerves were replaced with unsettling fear. They had Carrie. Whoever *they* were. Molly wouldn't hurt her, surely. Then again, Greysen didn't know who this Molly was. The Molly who had gone through so much since he'd left. The one seemingly controlling the show...

He hadn't thought about that until now. And he had no weapon. The sinking feeling churned in his stomach. He punched the gear shift into drive and pulled out from the parallel parking spot.

TWENTY

GREYSEN

reysen raced back to the Humavision IT building as fast as he dared to drive, clenching the steering wheel with white-knuckled hands. He pulled into a front parking spot and jumped out of the seat, the car door left ajar as he ran back into the Humavision IT building. He stared down the receptionist, who pointed left without opening her mouth.

He turned left and followed the voices back to the room he'd used the Memory Machine in and pounded his fist on the door. He backed up, his heart racing in anticipation of what he'd find next. *Wish I had my gun…* Perhaps he could pass down the hall and go to the first-aid room to retrieve it. *There's no time.* There was nothing to do but plunge into the situation, thoughts and anxieties aside. It was time to get to the bottom of this, once and for all.

The door opened.

Greysen barged in, taking in the room at a glance. The person who had opened the door looked like he could have been twins with the gangbanger face-tattooed messenger in Chicago. His beard wasn't as thick, but he fit the part of the muscle. The other guy, who sat next to Carrie on a fold-out chair, did not look like those two, however.

He was clean cut. Wearing a suit. Young and attractive. It looked like he might have just walked out of the stock market exchange.

"Someone want to tell me what the hell is going on?" Greysen barked. His nostrils flared. As he glanced over his shoulder at the man who shut the door behind him, his nails bit into his palms.

The person in the suit crossed his arms and smirked. "Greysen Price. Nice to officially meet you. I think you'll be a lot easier to work with than some previous colleagues." He lifted his chin, clearly confident in that declaration.

"Yeah, well, your thoughts are wrong," Greysen growled. He clenched his fists. "What's going on here? Money laundering through Humavision? Is there more to it than that? How many of these poor people have you involved?" He threw his hand up, gesturing to the others.

Let's see... there's the receptionist up front who clearly knew something was going on. Molly, of course. And now Carrie...

Where is Molly now?

The young guy stood, screeching his chair back on the linoleum.

Carrie retracted, wincing.

Greysen's heart weakened at the sight. *What has she been through because of me?*

"Well see that's for me to know and you to find out." The man smirked.

Greysen crinkled his nose when he caught a glimpse of a gold tooth between the man's lips. His eyes wavered and he saw the duffle bag of money next to the chair the guy stood from.

"Oh that? Yeah. You were makin' me nervous runnin' around the whole damn city with my money in your car, so I had one of my guys—" He nodded to one of the musclemen. "—retrieve it for safekeepin'."

"Why'd you make me bring it here?" The words left Greysen's mouth before he could stop himself.

He laughed under his breath. "Let's call it a test, if you will."

"I'm not doing this bullshit con with you like Edrick did, if that's what you're thinking. It's over." Greysen's throat was dry. He reached up

269

and touched his neck a moment. He'd give anything for a drink of water.

"Oh I've got a few reasons why you will." The man clicked his tongue and nodded over to the man on his left, who raised a gun at Greysen.

Carrie audibly gasped.

Greysen held up his hands; his eyes the size of saucers. *They're not going to shoot me. They need me!* Every muscle tightened in his body; his heart raced. Just when he was about to shut his eyes tightly to block out what was about to happen, a voice erupted behind him, in the frame of the door. He hadn't even heard it open again.

"You don't want to do this, Lucio."

Greysen turned to look into the eyes of Molly Green. A crossfire of emotions surged through him. Here she was.

Betrayer.

He spoke before he could stop himself. "You're a liar!" he spat at her. "I knew you were their leader!"

The man she'd called Lucio cackled. "Ha! Molly, dear… so glad you could join us. I was just about to hit you up. Didn't know you were also in KC, baby girl."

"Shut up!" she hissed past Greysen. Then she looked back to him, her expression grave. "Grey,

I'm not—I have nothing to do with these bastards." She glared at the muscleman, who still had his gun trained on Greysen. "And you, put that down. Nothing good will come from that."

"What will you do for me if I decide we don't kill him right here and now?" Lucio asked, and he squinted over at Molly with that confident smirk.

"Oh you think you're fly, huh?" Molly snapped. "This ends here, right now. Whatever you had going with Edrick, he's dead now, okay? He's gone. What business do you have with this man?" She motioned to Greysen.

Greysen tried to follow what was happening, back and forth between Molly and Lucio. He was frozen in place, information entering his mind at an exponential rate.

Molly's not their leader? He'd called her a liar to her face. He'd thought so many bad things about her.

He'd been wrong all along about her, too.

She'd only been there to help him?

"Oh okay, well maybe I'll just kill you too, then." Lucio pulled a gun from inside his jacket and pointed it at Molly.

Carrie screamed, covering her ears and shying away.

271

Molly's face tensed, and she slowly moved into the room, away from the doorway. "You're going away for a long time," she whispered as she slowly sank to her knees.

Lucio cocked his head and furrowed his brow. "Oh and to answer your question, looks like neither of you are in for taking Crowder's place. I lost a guy in my operation, and I need a body to replace him that's *trustworthy*." He clicked his tongue behind his teeth. Then he turned his gun sideways, still pointed at Molly.

She put her hands up in defense, but kept her glare fixated on Lucio. "What operation?"

"You already know wha—"

"Just say it. I just..." She caught her breath and continued, "Greysen needs to hear what the operation is, so he fully knows what he's turning down. Perhaps he just... doesn't understand." She stole a wide-eyed glance over to Greysen, then back to Lucio.

Lucio narrowed his eyes, then turned to Greysen, his gun wavering in his grip. "We print money. You wash it. Edrick's been a cover for years." He shifted his weight from one foot to the other.

Greysen inhaled sharply. "Is that why—" his voice cracked. "Is that why he killed himself?"

"The business ain't for everyone, my man."
Lucio grinned.

Greysen looked over at Molly who, on her
knees, squeezed her eyes shut. *What the—*

"Freeze! Everyone on the ground. Drop your
weapon!"

It all happened so fast. Greysen hit the
ground at the shouted order and covered his
ears, pressed his cheek into the floor. With a
thundering pulse, his eyes darted at ankle level.

So many noises. So many feet surrounding
him.

"Hey, you!"

Someone grabbed the sleeve of his jacket
and yanked it. He peeked up into the light to see
an officer instructing him to back up to the wall.
He scrambled to his feet and followed their
orders, finally allowing himself to view the scene.

It was an entire raid. A whole police force.
They'd already disarmed and taken down Lucio
and his muscleman partner. Molly was gone.
Greysen looked to his left to see Carrie up
against the wall, too, her face in a daze
watching   people   do   their   jobs.

"Hey! You okay?" He whispered over to her.

She broke her stare and turned toward him,
then nodded quickly.

Greysen looked back to the police as they hauled a handcuffed Lucio to his feet and escorted him from the room, followed shortly after by the muscleman, also in cuffs.

They'd probably been following a lead for a while on these guys, these most-likely-highly-wanted players in the money-laundering game. Or whatever game they were playing at, trying to rope Greysen and his company into.

"Mr. Price?"

He turned to face one of the policemen.

"We'll need you to come to the station for some questioning. I understand your receptionist at the front desk here can provide us with information on every employee you have?"

Greysen nodded. "Yes, anything you need."

"Are you able to meet us there or would you like an officer to escort you?"

Greysen looked over at Carrie.

"We will also be questioning the other female witness and the Confidential Informant who were present here as well," the officer added.

Greysen nodded again. "I can make my own way there, no problem. I'm comfortable doing that."

The policeman nodded and turned to speak to someone there who looked to be working in evidence.

Carrie spoke up again in a soft voice. "I'm gonna..."

Greysen looked over at her.

"... take them up on the ride offer. They also want me to stop by the ambulance out front and see the medic."

"That's a good idea. You should do that." He rubbed his hands on his thighs as a sudden soreness emerged throughout his entire body. *I'm too old for all this...* "Carrie, I'm so sorry, for what I've put you through."

She shook her head. "It's fine. Greysen, you're the best boss I've ever had, okay? Don't doubt that. I'll uhh find my way back and I'll see you in Chicago, Boss. Okay?"

He scrambled to offer her a ride back home like the way they came, but her tone sounded confident. Perhaps she didn't need his assistance back home, or want it for that matter. He nodded, half smiling.

She started toward the door. "You should go..." She tilted her head toward the hall, where he caught a glimpse of Molly standing against the wall outside. Then, Carrie left, moving down the hall in the opposite direction, through a sea of first responders and KCPD.

Greysen didn't hesitate, leaving the room as he caught Molly's attention. "Can we... talk?"

His voice trembled. He didn't even try to steady it.

She nodded and led the way.

He followed her through the hall to the front of the office, to the outside. An ambulance sat to the left, along with a parking lot full of emergency and police vehicles. A bench sat off to the side of the building's front for smokers, and they headed for it.

Greysen waited for her to sit, then followed her lead.

He'd waited for this moment for so very long. And yet it was so different from what he'd been imagining this whole time. *Where do I even begin...?* "I'm sorry I called you a liar. I thought..." He laughed under his breath, embarrassed. "I thought you were the leader of that entire operation." His cheeks flushed.

She half-smiled. "I'm not sure if I should be flattered or offended." She sounded amused. "I did..." She cleared her throat. "I was involved in some of their operation early on. Edrick had tricked me. I tried to follow his lead after you disappeared, felt I had no choice, really, until it went way south." She moved a ringlet out of her eyes, her gaze set on the pavement. "I wasn't just dealing with Edrick anymore. And I'd found out the money being washed was counterfeit. I

276

originally just thought he was having me move funds. But after I found out... I distanced myself. I got out."

"They always say that nobody ever gets 'out'," he interjected.

"You're right. And it's haunted me all these years. Always looking over my shoulder for one of Lucio's guys to come after me. Or the other side. Afraid that the cops would find out and pin me. So I decided to go to the cops myself."

Greysen cocked at eyebrow at the realization as though a lightbulb had gone off above his head. "So that's why you prompted this Lucio guy to actually say what he was up to?" He stabilized himself with both hands on the bench.

"I needed a confession. They waited to move in until we got that. I didn't even know you'd be there in the room when I got there." She closed her eyes and shook her head.

"Carrie..." he breathed.

"Well I know that now." She looked up and smiled.

Greysen stifled a small laugh, reaching up and scratching the back of his head. "I thought you were trying to take the CEO role away from me. I thought you wanted to be the head of Humavision."

She turned to him. "Grey. *You* are the head of Humavision. Me? I'm fighting my own fight. I've been on my own journey since I left the company years ago." She rubbed the back of her neck a moment.

"What about the locket?" Greysen asked. "Dot said you'd gone asking her about it. You are the only person I ever told about that chip. How did you know I sent it to her?"

She scoffed and shook her head. "I didn't. But when I came to your apartment to talk about losing yourself in the memories... I wasn't just there to warn you."

"You brought up the DNA invention then."

"I didn't know that you'd even hidden it, or where. But then you mentioned Dottie... and I just knew. I had to look into it." She shrugged. "Of course I wanted to know where you had it, Greysen. You used my DNA in the prototype. I've seen the privacy that others have lost when they send their DNA to these ancestry companies. But I also know the invention would have been so helpful for DNA transplants to those that have genetic deformities. Why didn't you ever pursue it?"

He looked down. "You know why. Look at my history. Just when it could change the world for the better... it could also be used to clone people against their will, among so many other negatives. I had to hide it. Especially when I thought I was losing control of the company." He looked up at her and smirked. "I thought... I thought you'd betrayed me and were seeking it for yourself. For you or for who you were working for. I'm sorry, that's just how I felt..." He shifted uncomfortably.

Molly shook her head and scoffed.

He continued, "So back when Edrick was questioning Dottie in one of his memories, he really just wanted to know where I was. He couldn't have known about the locket."

Molly let out a sigh. "No, he didn't know about it."

Greysen reached his hand up to his chest as though placing it there would help calm the pulsating in his chest. He'd thought he'd hidden it in the perfect place by giving it to Dottie, someone who was trustworthy, yet oblivious to its worth. She'd been his first, and he realized now that he'd made a mistake by putting it in her care, regardless of her knowledge of its contents.

Molly looked away, then spoke again. "I didn't think you'd have told Dottie Rubec about the chip," she whispered. "She just thinks it's a necklace. A keepsake. And she lost it, anyway."

279

"We're better off with it at the bottom of the ocean." Greysen looked to the pavement. Well, he felt like shit now. Molly had been trying to protect herself by getting the chip back. Not put Dottie in danger. Not use it against his will or try to take the company away from him. And he believed her. Of all the mistakes he'd made in his life, and all the people he'd once trusted who had done him wrong, he had to believe Molly. He just had to. It was all he had left.

Exhaustion clouded his mind. He pressed his palms into his eye sockets before he looked into Molly's face. He'd been so grateful to get the opportunity to talk with her. But something tugged in his mind and felt like a boulder on his chest.

He cleared his throat. "Before we say goodbye, Moll, I just—I just have to ask you one thing," he started.

She adjusted her seat.

"If I'm going to be rewriting my history, then I need to know that one thing for sure was real... despite everything." He looked her longingly in the eyes, his cheeks flushed.

She cut him off. "Greysen... This—" she moved in closer to him on the bench. Closer to him than she'd been in a very long time, "—was real. Fate took us in different directions, but what we *had*,

I will never forget. It will always be a part of me."
The look in her eyes proved to him that she was confident and at peace with her decision.

He nodded. It was the perfect thing she could have said to give him the closure he so desperately desired.

After this day, he would go back to work. He would run that company to the best of his abilities, with the mindset of creating inventions that could help others. Because in the end, after everything he'd been through, that was what was left for him to live for. He could live for his ideas, the ones that helped make humanity better. The privilege he possessed to bring forth those ideas and inventions. Turning an idea into something tangible. Making the world a better place.

Relationships had never been his thing.

It was the work; the work gave him fulfillment.

And as he sat on that bench with the once love-of-his-life, the one he'd never end up with, that was okay.

People gained fulfillment from different things. He would focus his attention back on his work and stop chasing a dream he would never have—one that just wasn't in the cards for him.

There was just one other thing he needed to do first.

When they got back to Chicago, he was going to meet with Carrie to talk about how they could bury the Memory Machine project. Forever.

The world is not, nor will it ever be, ready for that one. Just the thought was elating. The Memory Machine had been a mistake. He'd lost himself in them—the false, biased memories. Wallowing in the past, trying to gain any new information from it, had been the biggest mistake of all.

And after that, there would be nothing left for him to chase. Nothing for him to long for. All that was left for him now was to mourn the loss of the life he'd thought he had, and live the life he'd been given.

TWENTY-ONE

PARKER

Mr. Greysen Price,

What a wild ride, huh? I am writing you this letter to let you know that after we had reconnected, I began to write the sequel to The Idea Man. But the book took a turn. I stopped writing your reality and began to write your nemesis.

You were power hungry.

You were out to get me.

You were toxic for my family. And I was going to show the world, through my writing, the man you truly are.

But in the midst of it all, I lost the man that I truly am. I don't write to ruin people's lives. Just as I've learned you don't invent to ruin people's lives.

Truth is, I've had the adventure of a lifetime since the moment you came into my life.

Please take this letter as a document of my resignation from Humavision, Inc. I appreciate the effort you put up to give me a chance to be something. But it's time for me to move on.

I'm sorry things didn't turn out the way you thought with our relationship. But hey, thanks for the identity crisis. It helped shape me into the man I am today. Some people don't have a relationship with their father, or are orphans. For a short time there, I had two dads. And that was pretty cool.

Thanks for watching out for me, man. I'll see you in another life.

Parker Rubec

TWENTY-TWO

PARKER

Parker pulled into his parents' driveway. He got out of the car and headed for the house, glancing quickly over the lawn with a heavy heart. It had been the scene of his identity crisis earlier this week.

Noriana was back at the hotel, sleeping in and packing their things for the long flight back to Paris, where they'd decided to continue to live. He needed this time alone with his family before heading back overseas, and she had been grateful to give it to him.

His dad answered the door.

"Hiya, Pops." Parker closed his arms around his father as he crossed the threshold.

"Coffee in the kitchen." Davis smiled and moved out of the way for Parker.

285

It hadn't taken Parker long to forgive his father for his deception. One thing was clear: he was protecting his wife. Parker had learned later, after the event on the lawn, that his dad had known about the relationship Dottie had had with Greysen, and about her miscarriage when she was a teenager.

He'd known they'd conceived Parker not too long after that, and more recently, he'd known Dottie had used a private account to book a plane ticket to Cabo. After Molly had come aggressively questioning, Dottie and Davis researched into her ex's current whereabouts. From the information they found regarding the accusation of Greysen kidnapping a child, as well as the status of Humavision now, she'd had to get away from a potentially hairy situation regarding her connection to him. They'd both known Greysen Price had some serious connections and enemies these days, and they needed to stay as hidden as possible until it blew over.

It was hard to stay mad at him to any degree.

Parker went into the kitchen and grabbed a mug. "You know if Mom's ready yet?" he asked over his shoulder.

"She'll be down soon. She's really looking forward to breakfast with you before you take off," Davis said, walking into the family room to catch the news on television.

"Hey man," Stephen said as he entered the kitchen and went for the coffee pot. He wore his usual physician scrubs and had dark circles under his eyes.

"Do you ever go home?" Parker joked to his brother.

Stephen didn't live at their parents' house. He had a beautiful wife and home to go back to. "I'm working a double this evening. This was closer to the hospital than driving all the way back home. And what gives?" He poured steaming coffee into a mug, then reached over and poured some into Parker's as well.

"Hey, I'm actually glad you're here, I've been meaning to talk to you one-on-one for a moment," Parker said as they both worked their way to the table.

"Yeah?"

"Look, Stephen. Thank you for finding Mom." He sipped his coffee, enjoying its strength and nutty aroma.

Stephen shook his head. "She wasn't missing."

"Yeah, but you hired that PI which evidently led to Mom coming home. How'd she find out about the tickets to Cabo anyway? Did you guys end up going to the warehouse I told you about?" He took another sip of coffee to lubricate his throat.

Stephen sighed. "Yeah. So Priya discovered Mom's ID was missing and found out the cops had known about that already, which is why they ruled it as her taking off. But the PI still wanted to cover all bases. So after we got home from checking out that creepy as shit warehouse in the West Bottoms, Mom was already here. She'd come home on her own because Dad reached out to her and stressed how seriously worried everyone was getting and that he was going to buckle." He leaned back in his chair.

"You did good, Stephen. You didn't give up, on any of us." Parker nodded at his brother and took another sip.

"Well I appreciate that."

Parker cleared his throat and shifted in his seat. "Hey, I wanted to ask you something."

Stephen's brow furrowed. "Spit it out, you're freaking me out, Parker. What the hell."

They both laughed.

"Uhm, so before all this started... I asked Noriana to marry me." He lifted his chin up and looked Stephen in the face. He bit his lip before parting his lips into a smile.

"What?" Stephen pushed his chair back and stood, his eyes wide and his smile even wider.

Parker stood to match him, nerves coursing. He shook out his hands. "I wanted to know if you'd stand up there at the altar with me when I marry my beautiful fiancé. Will you be my best man?" He looked down a moment into his mug before leveling eyes with his brother once more.

Stephen rounded the kitchen table and outstretched his arms for an awkward brother hug. "I'm honored. Truly. Of course I'll be your best man."

Parker nodded, elated at Stephen's response. Excited to share it with Nori. "Can you get enough time off work to come to the French countryside?"

"Hell yeah. Have you told Mom and Dad?"

Parker scratched the back of his neck and shook his head. "Nori and I are going to tell them together before we leave. It'll be hard to keep quiet during breakfast." He sheepishly laughed.

"Good morning, boys." Dottie came into the kitchen.

Parker avoided her gaze and sat back down awkwardly, as though he'd fallen into the chair. He shook out of it with another sip of coffee and looked up. He'd been relieved to see she was dressed and ready to go, as opposed to being in her robe, which would have been a possibility had his dad not told her Parker was coming early to take her to breakfast.

"Are you joining us, baby?" She came over to the table and kissed Stephen on the head as though they were still little boys.

"Ah no, Mom. Just you guys. I gotta get going. Thanks for the coffee." He finished off his mug, pushed the chair back, and headed out of the room, but not without shooting Parker a wink before he left. That unspoken brotherly bond where they didn't need words to know what they wanted to communicate.

Parker stood and placed his mug in the sink. "All set?" he asked her.

"Yes, let me just grab my purse."

They had a nice talk about nothing in particular as he sopped up some runny egg yolk with his toast. He was on his second cup of coffee as he listened to her in a daze.

"And that white yappy dog is always digging underneath the fence! Your father even tried to plant bushes in front of it but that did nothing."

Parker half smiled at her, grateful for the normal conversation. For the slow change of pace. It was a sense of ordinary calm that filled his belly along with the eggs and toast.

She paused for a minute, studying her own almost-empty plate before looking up to him again with a soft smile. "Look, Parker... I just want to thank you for being so concerned when I was gone. I feel so bad I couldn't tell any of you guys, but I didn't want to pull anyone else into it if I didn't have to. I didn't know the extent of your involvement at all. I'm just so, so sorry you had to go through that, and I feel responsible." She put both hands up on the table.

"It's okay, Mom. Really. I know. I understand. I'd have done the same. I'm just glad something terrible didn't happen to you. If anything ever happened to you, I'd be wrecked. We all would." He placed his hand over hers for a moment before retreating and taking another bite of his toast.

Her eyes welled up.

His throat tightened. He hadn't meant to make her cry. Especially not here, in the small diner they ate breakfast in.

"You're just a wonderful son and I couldn't have asked for anything more from my first-born."

He smiled. He'd come a long way from the beginning, when he'd left for Paris the first time. When he thought back to his life before, working a dead-beat job and hating it, not knowing where life would take him, it was crazy to see where he was now and realize all the stuff that had happened from point A to point B.

"And I'm just so proud of you," his mom continued. "Noriana is so beautiful and you two make a perfect pair."

He squirmed, bursting with his news. *Save it... save it for when Nori and Dad are here too.* He wiped toast crumbed from his mouth with the back of his hand. "Thank you, Mom. You know I love you." He was sincere. He meant it. She had given him everything.

She leaned back in the booth. "I... I wanted to wait until just before you were leaving to give you something."

He cocked his head to the side. "Oh? You didn't have to get me any gifts."

"I know. But this is important, and I think you should have it." She reached into her jacket and pulled out something that fit in the palm of her hand. She stretched her arm over the table towards him.

Parker moved a glass syrup bottle out of the way and met her hand in the middle, holding his palm out flat.

She gently placed the object in his hand.

It was a dainty tarnished chain, and all the way down at the end of it, a heart locket.

292

He wasn't sure what to say or do, but he felt the weight of the locket's intention in his hand.

"I want you to have it," she said quietly. Her eyes were vibrant, piercing into him.

"I thought..." His throat caught. "I thought you lost it?"

"I've had it right where it's needed to be this whole time. And now, *you* will hold the key."

He pulled it back to his chest. "I... I can't... I can't keep this in my possession, Mom."

"Yes, you can. Hold it dear. And if and when you ever need to use it—well, then you will have it. If not, then it's in the safest place it could possibly be."

It was as though the end of her sentence was the end of the argument, and that was that. His mom had a way of ending conversations that way. Having the last word.

He looked down at the locket, the one possession that Greysen wanted to keep safe, that he thought was lost forever, in the palm of his hand.

He'd put it away. Far away.

Everything that had happened at the Humavision IT building, and the lawn in front of his parents' house, had settled. Things were good now. Things were getting back to normal.

Nobody needed to find this locket with the chip in it. Nobody would know that he had it.

Except his mother, of course.

He put the locket away in his pocket as gently as he could. So many people had fought over what he now possessed. His family had gone through hell because his mother fled from feeling threatened by this very locket.

But Parker? He was going to stow it away to never be found. He was going to finish eating his breakfast with his mom, then drive back to the hotel where his beautiful bride was waiting to be taken back to their home in France, where they would begin the first days of the rest of their lives. Of course only after sharing with his parents that they'd intended to fly them out to the French Countryside for a Rubec wedding.

Or so he could only hope it was that easy, like the stories that would flood from his mind, through the pen and to the page.

Only in real life... it never was.

THE END

A NOTE FROM
THE AUTHOR

Dear Reader,

Thank you for taking the time to read the
continuation of Parker and Greysen's story.

If you've enjoyed this book, please help others
find it by writing a review on Amazon
or Goodreads. This is the number one best way to
show an author you enjoyed their work.

And as always, thank you for being on this
journey with me.

Kristin Helling

ABOUT THE AUTHOR

Kristin Helling enjoys stories with a journey—whether it's a journey across the globe, a journey through space, or a journey of finding one's self.

She writes primarily adult fiction thrillers. She's published a standalone Sci-fi thriller called *Capsule*, and a 4-book crime thriller series called the *Mastermind Murderers*. When she's not killing people (fictionally, of course!), she also has a passion for children's stories and writes them under the pen name Kristin Alis.

Kristin owns a coffee house in Kansas City MO, co-owns the publishing imprint Wordwraith Books, is married to a Photographer, and is Mama to one little boy and his hairy sibling, a collie-shepherd mix.

Find more books by Kristin Helling at
www.kristinhelling.com

Sign up for bonus content at
www.kristinhelling.com/jointhejourney